I0733548

Cover Design: Deranged Doctor Designs
Editing: Trusted Accomplice

CHAPTER 1

Patrick O'Malley released a savage curse as he rolled to a sitting position. It had been a solid year since he returned from the Otherworld, reborn as it were, after a grisly death at the hands of his greatest enemy.

Loman O'Connor.

Thank the Goddess that scaldy gobshite was no more.

Patrick would've grinned if it wouldn't have hurt so badly.

Which brought him back to his current predicament. One year later, and his body hadn't healed properly. Nor had his magic completely returned. Both oddities in and of themselves.

And wasn't that the rub? He'd gone through life without anything remotely like abilities, only to experience the brief euphoria of the epic power his ancestors took for granted before it was stolen by those fecking O'Connors a second time. Yes, he could perform a few basics, like conjuring food and teleporting when need be, but that was about the extent of it.

Glancing around the cheerful room of the Black Cat Inn, he grimaced. His daughter Bridget had created a clean, comfortable atmosphere for visitors, but all Patrick saw were memories of the home he'd shared with his faithless wife, Rose. They seemed to be the only memories that actually stuck of late.

The best thing to come of his marriage was his five children. But they were all grown now, and he'd missed almost the entirety of their lives. And didn't that sadden him?

A knock at the door roused him from his maudlin thoughts.

"Da?" Bridget called out. "Will you be coming down soon, or do you want me to conjure a tray for ya?"

It appeared his eldest was trying to make up for lost time in the only way she knew how—caring for him, as she did everyone.

"I'm grand, Bridg, me love," he hollered back. "I'll be down in a bit, yeah?"

"Sure, and I'll have your breakfast ready."

Patrick met his tired forest-green eyes in the dresser mirror. Once, when he'd been happy, they'd shone like the emeralds in a queen's tiara. But that had been many betrayals ago, and he wasn't the optimistic fool any longer. No, things like hope were for the young. All he had were memories he'd prefer to forget.

He sighed.

Soon enough he'd need to tell Bridget he was leaving again. He had more of Loman's victims to search out and help emotionally heal if he could. Or so the Goddess Anu had told him was his mission. And wasn't it a good thing? Because if he didn't keep busy, he'd lose what was left of his bleeding mind. The fecking thing was no better than Swiss cheese on a good day, with its big gaping holes. He'd always hated that shite, with its sharp flavor, leaning towards bitter—not unlike him.

Burning started along the skin of his forearms, and he released another vicious curse. It had been ever the same since the day he cooked his limbs and face in his attempt to save his youngest daughter, Dubheasa, from Loman. Despite the fact he was thoroughly healed in the physical sense, the neurotransmitters in his brain preferred to misfire when the mood took them and cause him to relive the agony of that day. Worse than the burning sensation was the occasional piercing phantom pain from the godforsaken crossbow bolt Loman had buried in his chest.

Black rage clouded Patrick's vision before he could get a handle on the emotion. His anger issues were at an all-time high these days, and it didn't take much for him to snap.

If he could stand the sight of the man, he'd call Ronan O'Connor and ask the Guardian for help. But he couldn't and wouldn't. Ronan resembled his father, Loman, and Patrick had difficulty accepting he wasn't a snake in their midst. Only for Dubheasa would he be civil. She loved the fecker. Her *supposed* fated mate.

Only, Patrick knew there was no such thing. Hadn't Rose proven that?

With a massive eye roll and another grimace, he climbed to his feet.

"Get it together, Paddy," he told himself. "You've a bleedin' job to do."

Shuffling across the room, he lifted a small journal and flipped to the bookmarked page. Yesterday, with the weight of failure heavy on his soul, he'd lined out another name. The victim's sister said the man had vanished less than two days ago. No goodbye. Not a single indication he'd intended to leave other than a couple of paranoid episodes. And sure, wasn't the family reliving the puir bastard's disappearance from last year when Loman had used him for his magical fuel?

His wasn't the only one. Those disappearances seemed to be happening with more and more frequency. A select few ex-prisoners had found it too difficult to integrate back into their old lives. Their families could never understand the trauma they'd suffered, and discussing it with anyone who hadn't lived it... Well, it was simply too hard to form the words.

Frustrated he'd been too late to make a difference, Patrick blew out a breath and scrubbed his palms up and down his face, absently noting he needed a shave. After conjuring a cup of strong black coffee, he guzzled half of it, barely caring about the burn to the roof of his mouth and tongue. Neither was anywhere close to what he'd gone through with his arms and face after sticking his hands through the electrified bars to strangle Loman. His only regret was that he hadn't succeeded. Maybe Dubheasa wouldn't have died in such a horrid way if he could've held on longer. Granted, she'd possessed the key to leave the Otherworld, and she'd taken him with her when she escaped, but he'd have saved her the pain of a grisly death if possible.

Another knock sounded.

"Jaysus, Bridget!" he snapped. "I told ya I'd be—"

The wooden door swung back on its hinges, and Ronan crossed the threshold, expression grim. "Paddy—"

"What the feck do *you* want, O'Connor?"

"For myself, not a bleedin' thing. Anu, on the other hand, wants a progress report."

"Well, I don't have one, so you can feck all the way off, yeah?"

Ronan's silvery stare turned hard as diamonds, and his jaw looked to be made of granite. "Hate me if you must, Patrick O'Malley, but I'm not your enemy. That was Loman, and he's gone."

"Aye, and you're the spitting image of the man. You can't be telling me the apple falls far from *that* cursed tree! Rotten, the lot of ye!" His anger gave him strength, and he stalked over to Ronan. "And if you hurt my daughter in any way, you'll be answering to me, ya will."

"I'd lay down my life for her," Ronan said somberly.

The sincerity in his tone couldn't be denied, and a smidgeon of Patrick's burning rage cooled. How could he remain angry in the face of a revelation like Ronan's? The young man had begged Loman to save her—right before the bastard killed him to prove a point.

For a split second, Patrick experienced remorse.

No one deserved a father like Loman.

"He's as far from the rotten apple as you'll get, Da," Dubheasa stated as she entered the room to stand beside her man. "You've got to accept we love and trust him, yeah? Ronan has saved us time and again from his father. Are you unable to remember what happened on the island, then?"

"I remember," Patrick grumbled. But his faith had been broken many years ago by those close to him, so it was doubtful he'd ever trust the son of his lifetime enemy, even if he were so inclined. "You can tell Anu I'm after doing reconnaissance today. But damn me if a goddess shouldn't already know that."

Other than a thoughtful narrowing of his direct silvery gaze, Ronan remained silent.

"Don't you have children to watch?" Patrick waited a beat to rub it in. "A glorified feckin' nanny, ya are."

Anger flared to life in the Guardian's eyes, but still, he said nothing. Dubheasa, however, had plenty to say.

"You'll not be talking to him like that, Da. If you can't be civil, you'll shut your gob."

Although Patrick had been half serious with his jab, he didn't appreciate the way his daughter was quick to fight Ronan's battles. "Don't be disrespecting me, girl. I'm your da, and you'll—"

"I'll nothing! You weren't around to raise Eoin or me, so you'll have no say in what we do now." With a toss of her glossy black hair, she rested fisted hands on her hips, and with the exception of her emerald eyes, she was the spitting image of Rose.

His heart knew the difference, but he experienced a pang anyway.

"And respect is earned, Da. When you show you're deserving of it, you'll be getting it, and not a moment before." She elbowed her mate without turning her head to look at him. "And you can wipe that feckin' grin off your face, Ronan O'Connor."

Clearly, she had eyes in the back of her head. *Or* she knew the man better than Patrick suspected.

"Sure, and I can't help it, Dove," Ronan replied with a deep chuckle. "You've a fierce temper, and it sparks joy in my heart."

"Pfft. Go on with ya, then."

But her scowl softened, and her eyes lit with humor as she gazed up at him. In return, he stared down at her as if she were the moon to his stars. The two were mad for each other.

Patrick wanted to howl his anger and grief that she'd let a traitor into their lives, but she was right in the fact he had no voice in the matter. If he were being objective, he'd say the two of them made a beautiful couple. They'd made an even more beautiful baby.

"Where's Rory? I want to spoil my grandson," he said.

Ronan's eyes were marginally warmer when he looked away from Dubheasa and locked on Patrick. "You'll need to fight his Aunt Ro for the pleasure. She stole him from Dove the instant she arrived this morning."

"Tell her and Carrick to make their own. I'm to be the boy's favorite."

His teasing did what he'd intended, and Dubheasa laughed before kissing his grisly cheek.

"You need a shave and shower. When you're done, I'll be sure Roisin surrenders our gremlin to you."

"You're a good egg," Patrick said with a wink. "One with horrible taste in men, but I'll not be holding it against ya."

She rolled her eyes and shook her head before patting his cheek. "Keep it up, and you'll be blacklisted from the babysitter roster."

"There are worse things." As he knew all too well.

CHAPTER 2

"*Y*er brother's gone."

Fionola Bohannon closed her fatigued eyes. Her mother wasn't telling her anything she didn't know. Two nights ago, she'd gone to check on Tadhg only to find his flat ransacked and no trace of his whereabouts. She'd tried to keep it from her mother as long as possible, but like the proverbial saying, the cat was out of the bag.

Last year, her only brother had been abducted by Loman O'Connor. The evil fucker had randomly plucked and imprisoned members of the magical community, much like a scientist collecting rare butterflies, and he'd put them in cages. Tadhg was one of many held at a compound on a remote island off the coast.

The Aether, Damian Dethridge, along with a small contingent of his magnificently magical friends, saw to it that Loman was put down like the feral beast he was. This time, never to return.

Thank Anu!

But Tadhg was missing.

He didn't go willingly, based on the state of his flat.

"Did ya hear me, girl?" Mam demanded, her voice pitched to raise the dead.

"Yeah." Fi expelled a heavy sigh. "I'm after finding him, Mam. I've called that man who came around to help Tadhg. He'll be arriving today to see what he can uncover."

Face tragic and tears brimming in her large blue eyes so like Fi's own, Mam nodded. "That's grand, then." With her mouth pressed into a thin line, her mother patted her shoulder, smoothed down her apron, and shuffled her way to the stove.

When it came to confronting their troubles, the Bohannons excelled at total avoidance. Da would hang about the pub, and Mam would make enough food for the entire village. Fionola and Tadhg had learned from the best, and they, too, refused to discuss their feelings. Snarky comebacks and work kept the worst of their emotions at bay.

And having considered their inability to communicate, Fi realized Tadhg might be missing for that very reason. If he felt threatened or was scared someone was after him, he'd quite likely jackrabbited for the hills rather than give her the details. Even now, he might be burrowing in and hiding from the world.

Guilt or something similar crept in.

Fi should've pushed harder for her brother to speak to someone about his trauma. He wasn't all right, but she chose to believe him when he said he was. If the worst happened, it was on her. Scrubbing her palms over her face, she unfurled from a sitting position with a check of the clock.

Goddess, she was tired. But rest was for the wicked, and she had a shift to cover for Marta at the pub. And if her father was sober, she'd break the news about Tadhg to Da while she was there.

Within ten minutes, she was heading for the door.

"Are ya not eatin', then?" Mam demanded.

"I've got a shift. Marta's off to Dublin for the weekend."

"That feckin' girl's gonna find herself with a *ween* on her hip if she's not careful."

Fi hid a grin. "She's careful, Mam. Marta's not interested in a life like ours. She's got grand plans, she does."

"Aye. Too grand, if ya ask me."

Fi kissed her mother's cheek. "Is there any such thing as too grand? I'd take a villa in the south of France and be happy for it."

A twinkle lit her mother's pale blue eyes. "You're as batty as Marta."

"Sure, but I'm better at hiding it." Slinging her bag over her shoulder, Fi reached for the door handle. "Do you want me to send Da home?"

"Nah. Let him drink until he's pickled his liver. What care I?" Mam's snappy response lacked heat. In truth, she loved her husband, flaws and all. And who didn't have flaws?

Feeling particularly sentimental, Fi paused to say, "I love you, Mam. I've not said it enough, but I do."

Gesturing with her chin, Mam said, "Hurry now, girl. You'll be late for work."

"Is that your way of telling me you love me, too?" Fi asked dryly.

"And haven't I kept ya fed all these years, you ungrateful child?"

Laughing, Fionola whipped open the door and stopped short when she saw the visitor on the other side. Although she felt like a proper eejit, all she could do was stare at the man who had his fist raised to knock.

Tall, but not overly so, he had piercing green eyes and graying auburn hair. She couldn't tell the shape of his body, whether dad-bod or fit, because he was swathed in a navy blue peacoat. Yet her overall impression was of a man who ran toward muscled. His expression was startled, but beneath the instantaneous reaction, there was a worn quality to his visage, as if he constantly fought fatigue and lost.

Her need to hug him to her breast and stroke his thick, close-cropped hair while assuring him it would all be okay was as strong as she'd ever experienced. Granted, she didn't know what his issues were or if they were on a larger scale than his ability to cope, but her desire to soothe was there, all the same.

"Well, what are ya waitin' on, girl—Oh!" Mam quickly wiped her hands on her apron and swung the door wider, allowing her to see their visitor better. "What are ya after, then?" she asked him.

As if he had all day, his disturbing gaze traveled the length of Fionola's body and returned to her face. A frown tugged at his brows.

She was proud when she finally rediscovered her voice. "Are you lost?"

With a shake of his head, he glanced between Mam and her. "I'm Patrick O'Malley. I've come about Tadhg Bohannon."

"It was me you talked to. I'm Fionola Bohannon. Tadhg's sister." Fi glanced at the wall clock and grimaced. "You're early, but I'm late for my shift. If you walk with me, I'll fill you in."

With another kiss to her mother's cheek, she pushed past Patrick and started down the path, leaving him to follow if he intended. He'd disconcerted her. When they'd talked on the phone, she gave him directions to the pub, intending to tell him what she knew during her break. How he'd found their house was no mystery, though. It only took asking anyone in town.

Patrick fell into step beside her, but remained silent for three of her seven-minute walk.

"It's a lovely sight," he finally said, gesturing with his hand to the view of the village below them.

Since she was already late, she stopped at the overlook and absorbed her favorite scene. The rain had let up, and the fields were rich in color, greener from a good soaking.

"It is," she agreed with a smile. "Is this your first time in this part of the country, then?"

"No."

She waited, but he didn't elaborate. With a shrug, she started down the road. "So, as I told you on the phone, my brother went missing."

"Aye. I've come to help you find him."

Her shoulders dropped in relief, and until that particular moment, she hadn't realized her tension was so high. "What more do you need to know other than what I told you last night?"

"I'd like to see his flat."

"Sure. I've a shift, but I'll get Da to take you if he's sober."

"Thanks."

Again, they fell into a comfortable silence as they traversed the road to the village. She had the ridiculous urge to clasp his hand, but shook it off.

"Are you married?" he asked in a gruff, seemingly seldom-used voice.

Fi jerked to a halt and gaped. It didn't take him long to realize she'd stopped, and he spun back to stare at her. His dark brows snapped together, and he opened his mouth as if he intended to speak, but clamped his jaw shut the next instant.

What the hell?

WHAT THE BLOODY *hell was wrong with him?*

Patrick didn't know what demon had possessed him, but he was prepared to battle the fecker to death if only to stop it from doing stupid shite on his behalf. Still, he made a visual sweep of her left hand, and the tension left his body when the lack of a wedding ring registered.

"Not married," she said with a clipped tone and a sassy toss of her strawberry-blonde hair, as if irritated he'd asked. Yet her gaze sought his left hand, and his inner demon prompted him to pull it from his coat pocket and wave it in the air.

"There's no commitment here, either."

Her lips quirked, but she didn't grace him with a smile as he'd hoped. "What matter is it of mine, Patrick O'Malley?"

"Just in case you were after knowing," he countered.

"Well, I'm not. *After knowing*, that is."

"Your eyes were."

"Shut your big gob! They weren't!"

He chuckled in the face of her indignation.

She hastened her already brisk pace, but he possessed a long stride and easily kept time with her.

"Do you think you'll be able to find Tadhg?" she asked, reminding him why he was there.

"I'll not lie and tell you yes, but I'm after doing my best."

She nodded, but her disappointment showed. Although he suspected, like any Irish person, she was a stone-cold realist, no one cared for bad news.

At the rate Loman's ex-victims were vanishing, it didn't bode well for Tadhg. But he kept that tidbit to himself.

"Do you think his disappearance is connected to the others? To Loman's island, somehow?" Fionola asked, as if she'd read his mind.

His heart resounded loudly in his chest, kicking up its pace until the thrumming in his ears was all he could hear. How had she learned about the other victims? He was doing a piss-poor job of keeping things under wraps if all of *Éire* knew what was happening. Grey spots danced in front of his eyes, and a wave of dizziness nearly knocked him down.

"Mr. O'Malley! Patrick!"

When her chilly hands cradled his face and her devastatingly blue eyes locked with his, Patrick came back to himself. Warm buzzing started within his cells, as if they were amping up for a teleport, yet his feet never left the ground.

"Aye. I'm grand, love. No need to fuss."

Fionola released Patrick faster than scalding chips straight from the oil, and nothing short of horror filled her face as she repeatedly shook her head.

Filled with dread, Patrick ventured a glance around, but nothing seemed strange.

Her voice was hoarse when she asked, "What was that? What did I see?"

CHAPTER 3

"*Y*ou'll have to explain it to me, love, because I've not seen anything out of the ordinary."

Fi stared at Patrick with horrified wonder. Was she going mad? How had he missed the scenery change? One second, the village was before them, but in the next, what appeared to be a glass-and-cinder-block cell had taken its place. She'd scarcely had time to register the change before the room disappeared. What the hell had she witnessed, and where had it gone?

"It was like a telly flickering from one station to another and back again," she explained as she tried to wrap her brain around the phenomenon she'd witnessed. "The village was gone. *Completely* gone."

His concerned expression sent the back of her wrist to her forehead to check for fever. Slightly warm, not overly so, and no reason to worry on that front. A broken mind was another matter entirely.

His wary look disturbed Fi, making her distrust what she'd seen. Checking the time, she sighed heavily. There was nothing for it. Work beckoned. As it was, she'd be late clocking in, and she'd be subjected to Noah's sour puss for the shift. Her boss did nothing to hide his anger when riled. Of course, he was carrying a grudge the size of *Éire* since their breakup, though he was the bleeding reason for it. Goddess forbid she even smiled at another man. The wanker would double her workload. She'd be damned lucky if he didn't fire her for being late again this week, and if she was any worse at her job, he would.

Jaysus, what she'd give to find Tadhg and get the hell out of this place! To go back to London and forget small-town life. Everybody was up in everyone else's business twenty-four-seven, and she was done with it.

"Where have ya been?" Noah ground out the instant she stepped across the threshold, cementing her latest opinion that he was a horse's behind.

After wiping his hands on the stark white towel across his deliciously rounded shoulder, he gestured with his stubborn chin toward the far side of the pub. He ran his fingers through his coal-black hair, mussing the thick strands, thereby waking her ovaries from a deep slumber for the second time today. One prodded the other, and together they dropped eggs in anticipation of an epic shagging, like in days gone by.

Fi pressed her palm low on her abdomen and sent them a silent signal to cease their foolishness. Noah Riley wasn't for the likes of her, despite how often his midnight eyes heated when they saw her. Or, like now, when they filled with ire as he noticed her handsome companion.

"Your da's pissed. Take him home, then get your arse back here, yeah?" With a frustrated glance at her father, Noah reached for another pint glass to fill.

"Don't talk to her in that tone, or you'll be facing my wrath," Patrick snarled.

Fi didn't know which of them was more surprised, Noah or herself. Even the piss-faced patrons of Noah's pub appeared stunned. The energy in the room turned dangerous on a dime, and the fine hairs rose over her entire body, similar to the disappearing-village incident earlier.

Placing a calming hand on Patrick's arm, Fi gave a little rub. "He didn't mean anything by it. It's Noah's way to be a bear."

Black brows clashed over eyes filled with consternation as her ex watched the two of them. The subtle shift of Noah's body indicated he was preparing for action should the need arise. Although not the most powerful warlock of her acquaintance, he possessed enough magic to defend himself and those present. He also wasn't opposed to underhanded means to subdue an out-of-control customer.

"Well, Noah the Bear needs to check his bleedin' attitude," Patrick growled. "That's not the way to talk to an employee."

Fi dropped her hand. She'd begun to feel particularly kindly toward him during his posturing, but her goodwill flew out the window the second he'd said "employee." Why the hell was she mentally drawing hearts around their initials when the man was simply viewing her as a pub worker, and not a woman to be protected? All because he'd asked if she was married?

And it wasn't as if she *needed* to be protected. She could damned well take care of herself! But that didn't mean she didn't appreciate a male going to the mat for her if he believed she'd been wronged.

"Sure, and you're right," Noah said as he slid a Guinness to a patron on his right. "And how would you be knowing how a boss talks to anyone? What's it you do?" Noah asked conversationally, walking around the end of the bar toward Fi's father. He didn't wait for an answer as he hoisted the burly James Bohannon to his feet with a grunt and scowl. "Have ya been packing on the pounds there, Jimmy?"

Da rubbed his belly and grinned. "Me Clara loves to cook, she does."

"And you don't miss a meal," Fi muttered as she positioned herself under one of her father's arms to help Noah. A smile curled his full lips, and she saw a flash of sparkling white teeth before he remembered they weren't friends anymore.

"I'll ring Katie for tonight, Fi," he said in a low voice. "Take care of your da and get that other fecker out of here. You know better than to bring your lovers in my pub. Especially one looking for trouble."

"He's not... We're not... No! I..." In her agitation, she released her father.

Noah's dark eyes narrowed. "You're not what?"

"Together," she replied in an equally low voice with a quick glance at Patrick, who happened to be watching them like a Peregrine Falcon summing up a rabbit for its next meal. Slipping her father's arm over her shoulder, she grimaced. "He's here to help me find Tadhg. And you don't give a shite about me or my lovers, all the same. So don't be pretending you do."

Noah stopped short, and she almost lost her grip on Da.

"Why would you be saying it like that?" His deep voice held incredulity, and his expression was dumbfounded, like she'd smacked him with a wooden plank. "Of course I give a shite!"

"You ended it, Noah. Not me. I—"

"Oh, for the love of Pete!" Patrick edged her out of the way and put his shoulder under Da's belly, hauling him up. The fact he was able to lift someone of her father's stature and size without staggering was impressive as hell. "I've things to do and don't plan to sit around all day listening to lovers' quarrel, to be sure."

"We aren't lovers!" Fi protested.

"We were," countered Noah, amusement heavy in his voice.

She spun to glare at Noah, and he backed up a step with his large, capable hands in the air. But the smirk on his stupid face was begging to be smacked off.

"Shut yer gob, Noah Riley!"

Patrick turned his back, but not before she saw him grin.

What was wrong with her that she found either of these

two eejits attractive? For the second time in less than thirty minutes, she pressed the back of her wrist to her forehead to check for a fever. Maybe her brains were slowly being eaten away by a deadly amoeba.

"You all right there, Fi?" Noah stepped forward and settled his palm against the skin of her forehead as she dropped her arm. "Are you feeling unwell?"

"I'm grand," she snapped, shoving him away in the process. "Just feckin' grand."

Again, his grin flashed. "Aye, ya are."

With a snarl, she turned to leave, but not before he clasped her elbow.

"So what is this about your brother?"

Had he not exhibited concern, she'd have stomped off, but his genuine caring for Tadhg halted her exit.

"He went missing. Sure, and he's been a touch off since the island, since, well, you know. But he always tells us when he needs to escape for a bit."

"What's the deal with him, Fi?" He nodded in the direction Patrick had gone. "Why bring him into family business?"

"He was a captive of Loman O'Connor's, too. I'm thinking if anyone can find Tadhg, Patrick O'Malley can."

Noah's expression turned thoughtful. "O'Malley? As in the Unlucky O'Malleys?"

"Well, I can't say I know about all that, but he came by about a month ago to check on Tadhg. Said he was contacting all Loman's victims to make sure they were adjusting to the real world after their ordeal." She shrugged. "He mentioned a few were having a rough go of it and went missing. It seemed best to call him when my brother disappeared on us."

"I'd have helped ya, Fi. You know that, yeah?"

It hurt to look into Noah's intense, dark eyes. She'd loved him once, and he'd broken her heart for no reason she could discern other than he didn't love her back.

"You've got enough on your plate, Noah." She offered up a smile, but it pulled down at the corners of her mouth. Not wanting to appear pathetic and sad, she shifted to leave again.

"Fionola." Her name was spoken achingly sweet, stopping her in her tracks, and the salt from unshed tears burned her lids.

"Please don't," she croaked. "I've got to keep it together until I find Tadhg."

He drew her into a hug, and the feel of his solid embrace was welcoming. "We'll find him, love. I promise."

"You can't promise me that, Noah. You didn't even know he was missing."

The soft black material of his shirt against her cheek shifted when he shrugged, and the sensation wasn't at all unpleasant. But it felt too fecking good to be held by him again, and she pulled away, then made the mistake of glancing up. An unidentifiable emotion burned in his eyes before he blinked it away and pasted on his standard devil-may-care grin.

"You're giving me mixed signals again," she accused with a scowl and a hard jab of her index finger against his forehead. "You'd best quit before you find yourself in my bed again."

"That wouldn't hurt my feelings in the least, love."

"It would hurt mine. The next person I shag will be someone who intends to commit to me." The single circuit wasn't all it was cracked up to be, and she was lonely in a way only a soulmate could ease.

"Fi—"

She pressed her palm over his mouth, ignoring the tingle it caused her nerve endings. "It's been almost seven months, Noah. You're only showing interest now there's another on the scene. And a stranger I've no connection to, at that." Dropping her hand, she stared at his beautifully formed mouth, which was a helluva lot easier than meeting his probing gaze. "Don't try marking a territory that's no longer yours to mark."

"What if I want it to be? Would you be willing to give me another chance?"

His question seemed heartfelt, but Fi wasn't prepared to consider what his about-face meant. Not when she had other pressing matters to attend.

"Are you coming, or am I expected to break my feckin' back by standing here all bleedin' day?" Patrick growled from the doorway.

CHAPTER 4

*P*atrick stole from his precious store of magic to teleport Fionola and her father back to their residence. He smothered a groan as he settled James on top of the man's bed. While there, he concealed any sign of weakness, both with his magic and his body, but if he didn't go soon, he'd give himself away.

Still, he needed to discover what he could about Tadhg Bohannon's disappearance before leaving. Unable to hide his limp this time, he followed Clara Bohannon back to the kitchen and eased into the chair she pointed to.

"What's wrong with you, then?" she asked matter-of-factly as she turned her back to set the kettle to a boil.

"Nothing."

"Sure, and that's the greatest load of malarky I've heard this week. And believe you me, I hear loads, I do. I'm married to *that* one." She gestured vaguely in the direction of the primary bedroom.

"Tell me about your son," Patrick said, in an attempt to deflect her attention away from what ailed him.

Clara half turned and narrowed her eyes as she studied him.

"Why are you hidin' your injuries? And why haven't ya been healed yet?" When he opened his mouth to protest her conclusions, she waved a wooden spoon, cutting him off. "I've birthed three children and have a man who lives for a pint or ten. Don't think to lie to me, Patrick O'Malley. I'll not have it in me house, I won't."

An unwitting smile curled his lips, and as soon as he realized he'd cracked his cool exterior, he sobered and shot her a glare. "Mind your own business, then, yeah? I'm here to find your son and not a mother."

"You're too bleedin' old to be any child of mine."

He scowled. "Jaysus, woman! You make me sound ancient!"

"Meh. If the shoe fits, you'll be wearing, to be sure."

From behind him, Fionola laughed. "Give the man a break, Mam. He brought Da home without complaint." With a light touch of his shoulder, Fi drew out a chair next to him and sat.

Oddly, Patrick didn't feel tired anymore. Around her, he seemed to receive larger bursts of energy and, with them, power boosts. Up close, she was lovelier than he'd first believed. Her skin was unblemished and glowed with health, pinkening when she noticed his admiring regard.

Although reserved, her gaze sparkled with life, and he couldn't help but recall how those eyes had snapped pure fire when she gave her boss what for. She'd denied an existing relationship with the man, but Noah Riley had claimed they were lovers once, and she'd blushed from neck to hair roots. They made a beautiful couple, him with his striking good looks and her angelic appearance. Darkness and light.

"Why did the pub owner end things with you?"

Hearing himself speak the low-voiced question shocked him, and he fought the urge to cringe. Yet the driving need to uncover the truth behind their relationship was stronger than his desire to remain detached. Although he told himself he didn't ever intend to fall in love again, he wasn't opposed to a steady shag. Fionola Bohannon would fit the bill if she was willing, unentangled, and preferred older men.

She gasped her surprise at his forwardness.

"And what business is it of yours, Patrick O'Malley?" Her tone was haughty, and her already wide eyes flared wider with ire.

Patrick's blood stirred. As if it had a mind of its own, his gaze zeroed in on her compressed mouth and refused to budge as his brain tormented him with all the possible ways he might tease a kiss from those delectable lips.

"Maybe I'm interested," he heard himself say.

Her flush darkened, spreading down her neck to the exposed V of her chest.

"I'm not," she retorted.

"Fair enough. I don't want what's not freely given." He nodded and, hiding his disappointment behind a blank expression, shifted to look at Clara. The elder Bohannon woman's knowing expression grated on his last nerve, and Patrick desired nothing more than to see the last of this house and the people in it.

"Tell me about Tadhg," he demanded again.

Fionola surprised him when she answered for her mother. "He's been haunted lately. It's the only way to describe it. Right, Mam?" At Clara's nod, she continued. "Always looking over his shoulder, as if someone were on his heels."

"He wasn't eatin'," her mother added.

"Aye, and it showed. He lost at least a stone, and he was haggard." Fionola bit her lip, and her hands were in constant motion as she poured herself a spot of tea and stirred in a spoon of sugar.

"He never mentioned any reason for his nervousness? Said someone was actually following him, then?" Patrick asked, curbing his urge to clasp her hands and steady her nerves.

"Not that I recall. Mam?"

Clara shook her head, cementing she was as clueless as her daughter.

"Do you know if he phoned anyone in the days before he went missing?" To be on the safe side, he'd have Dubheasa see what she could uncover on that high-end computer of hers. The girl was smarter than anyone he knew and possessed the skill to hack their government's database with one arm tied behind her back and a one-minute egg timer ticking loudly in her ear.

"No, but I've his provider's name. Does that help?" Fionola said.

"Aye."

He guzzled the last of his tea. What he wouldn't give for a shot of whiskey within its depths! Maybe he should stop by Noah Riley's pub for a few before heading to the Black Cat Inn. If he drank more than a pint or two in front of Bridget, he'd be subjected to one of her scoldings, and he had no mind to hear it.

Taking care with the cup and saucer, he set them on the table and climbed to his feet, barely managing to suppress a hiss of pain. His body reminded him of his age, and it felt battered, as if he'd fought a bull and lost. Surviving another excruciating day of aches without alerting the world to his plight was his aim.

Clearly, he hadn't succeeded in straightening without wincing, because both women frowned their concern, and Fionola reached out a hand to steady him. Without expression, he brushed her aside.

"Thanks," he muttered, refusing to make eye contact.

Rose had unmanned him. First with her taunts and affairs, and second when she'd joined Loman's team to make Patrick's life hell within the confines of the island prison. He'd been the victim once, and he wouldn't be weak in another person's eyes. Not physically. Not emotionally.

The world as a whole could fuck all the way off.

As Patrick limped his way toward the door, Fi shared a worried look with her mother. He was obviously hurting, but the stubborn jackass shunned her help. Mam had experience with mulish men, and Clara simply shrugged as she gathered the remains of tea to store for later.

Left with no choice, Fi followed Patrick outside.

"Do you think you can find Tadhg with so little to go on?" She hated that her voice cracked, but maybe if he understood her fear for her brother, Patrick might work harder to uncover his whereabouts. "What if he's come to harm?"

He turned so quickly she couldn't stop fast enough, and her chest pressed to his as one of his arms wrapped around her waist to steady her.

The breath whooshed from her lungs, and she stared up into his weathered face, still handsome despite any hardships. The green of his eyes lightened marginally as they locked with hers, and his lips twitched as if he wanted to smile or laugh. But standing in front of her was someone who refused to let his guard down. This much she sensed about him, over and above what she'd already witnessed by his actions.

"Who broke your heart, Patrick O'Malley?" she asked, whisper quiet.

His shutters came down, and the light left him. If he hadn't been holding her as gently as he was, Fi would've been terrified of the abrupt change. Cold. Lifeless. And a sneer bordering cruel.

"My wife," he replied in a clipped tone after what felt like the longest time. "Sure, and she liked to discover new ways to torment me daily."

When he didn't elaborate, Fi shifted her grip from his

shoulders to his face, cradling it between her palms. "She was a fool."

He softened. Not enough to invite confidences, but his terrifying look relented. A slight shift of his head pressed his lips to her skin.

"Thank you."

"You don't have to," Fi said. "I don't know a thing about you other than you volunteered your time to come here and search for my brother without expecting payment or praise of any kind. That alone tells me you're a good man."

A twinkle entered his eyes, and his mouth curled fully for the first time. His engaging grin stole her wits and made breathing difficult.

"Who says I'm not after payment?" His low, sexy timbre sent a shiver of delight throughout her body.

When he focused on her mouth, she licked her lips.

"I'm of the mind to collect with a kiss. Are ya willing?" he asked gruffly.

Her delayed comprehension was embarrassing, and his brow shot up as he waited for his comment to sink in. When it did, she blushed like the foolish schoolgirl she no longer was. Hell, she'd left crushes and girly sighs behind twenty-five years ago. At forty-three, she possessed enough experience to make their tame encounter laughable. Certainly not enough to draw attention from the censor police! Why, then, was she reacting as she was?

Regret twisted his mouth, and he dropped his arm. "I'll take that as a *no*."

But as he stepped back, her body reacted, willful and mindless to the bitter end. Taking the lead, she kissed him. The instant their lips connected, color burst behind her closed lids, and Fi experienced a sense of rightness. He sighed his pleasure into her mouth, and she drank it in, enjoying the heady sensation caused by his passion. What person didn't want to be desired?

Her arms snaked around his neck as her fingers burrowed into the hair above his nape, and locking his head in place, she tasted her fill of him. His wasn't the kiss of a young man, inexperienced and seeking. His held a lifetime of expertise, and that skill came into play as he languidly explored her mouth. Large, gentle hands traveled down her back until he reached the hem of her shirt, then explored underneath. His cool, skillful fingertips brushed along her spine, and she mewed as he leisurely stroked her like a cat, creating pleasure with every pass.

There was no accounting of time or space during their lengthy kiss. But if Fi had to say, it was a lifetime of perfection in the sum total of those moments they shared. When she dredged up the will to break away, she met his searing-hot gaze. His irises were the color of *Éire's* wet fields after a storm passed. Gorgeous and bright like the Emerald Isle she loved.

"It's the Goddess's honest truth when I say that's the best snoggin' of my life, and one helluva thank you." He brushed his thumb over her lower lip.

Laughing, she pushed him away.

"You've the Devil's own charm when you want to, Patrick O'Malley. And if I'm being true, I'd have to admit it was feckin' grand, too."

A mischievous light danced in his eyes. "Better than Ned Riley's?"

"Ned—oh, ya mean *Noah*," she corrected as if she hadn't caught on to his game. Scrunching her nose, she squinted. "I'll need more to compare. Maybe we should head back to the pub, and I could host a contest? The winner earns the title of best snogger and a night in my bed."

The teasing left him, and the distance between them was miles wide with no bridge for the gap.

"Patrick?" She touched his arm, but he jerked away. "What's wrong? Where did you find the hurt in the craic?"

The hand he ran through his hair trembled, and he stared at the village in the distance.

"Am I supposed to guess, then?" she asked. "Perhaps walk on eggshells around you from here on out?"

"No. It's sorry I am for taking the shine off a lovely experience. I'm a surly bastard, to be sure." His smile was self-deprecating, but the lighthearted man was gone.

"And it's sorry I am that your wife was a horrid creature to cause you such pain."

CHAPTER 5

The shared kiss with Patrick wasn't far from Fi's thoughts over the next few days, and the memory would disrupt her concentration at the oddest times. Noah's reserved demeanor had returned, and she put his thought-provoking question down to his nostalgia from their bed-rocking nights together. If their interactions were a little stilted and awkward, there was no cure for it.

From Tadhg, there was no communication, and it broke Fi's heart to think she might've done something to help him prior to his disappearance. It bothered her to assume his paranoia was a remnant of his time on Loman's island, but what choice did she have? She'd never seen a stalker or even a stranger in their midst.

Twice, she'd dreamed of Tadhg huddled alone in a cell, cold and hungry, with fear oozing from his pores as he cried out until he was hoarse. She was the one now haunted by nameless ghosts.

Texts to Patrick were met with blunt *yes* or *no* answers and no indication they'd ever shared an intimate moment. Yeah, and wasn't *that* the story of her life? It seemed hers was the kiss of death to any potentially interested party. After a snog or a hearty romp in bed, they scurried away, hurrying to move on to the next person, and Fi was left lonelier than ever, contemplating decades of mistakes.

With a self-pitying sigh, she collected the last of the emptied mugs and trudged on tired feet to the bar. Noah was waiting to accept the tray for washing up.

"You all right, love?"

She nodded in answer, too worn out to voice a lie.

As if he sensed her untruthfulness, Noah tossed down his towel and circled the counter. He clasped her hand and led her to the nearest bench, then urged her to sit as he straddled the seat, facing her. The action was reminiscent of the times when they'd dated, when he'd grip the wood and lean in to steal a kiss after making her laugh over some ridiculous remark or another.

Her heart pinged as she registered his serious demeanor.

"Are you firing me?"

"What? No!" He scowled and tipped her chin up to meet his eyes. "Fionola, listen to me, love. As long as you need it, there will be a place for you here."

She processed her relief by shutting her lids and slumping her shoulders. "Thank you."

"No need for all of that. Tell me what's happening with your brother. Any leads on Tadhg's location?"

"Not a one, and the not knowing is killing me, Noah. It truly is." Fi swept her hair away from her forehead. "I'm not sleeping well, and when I do manage a few hours, my dreams are filled with visions of him scared and alone."

She didn't tell him, when she wasn't worried about Tadhg, her sleep was also disrupted by hot-as-feck fantasies of being the center of a Noah-and-Patrick sandwich.

Knowing she'd give herself away if she looked at him, she

traced the wood grain on the bench seat. "I don't know what to do."

"No word from the Unlucky O'Malley?"

Surely he wasn't privy to her fanciful thought of the two of them, right? Heat crept up her neck, and she fought an urge to fan her warming face. "Very few."

"You'd have thought after a kiss like the one you shared with him, the man would be beating down your door to make ya his."

Fi's brows snapped together. How the bloody hell had he learned about it?

"I went to check on you after you left," he said, answering her unspoken question.

"I'm sorry if having witnessed it hurt your feelings, but I've stumbled across you and your lady of the week a time or two." Her tone was snippy, but hiding her jealousy wasn't something she was capable of at that moment.

"You've the right to do what you want with whoever you want, Fi. I'll not hold a kiss against you after I pressed pause on our relationship. But I'll be buggered if it didn't feel like salt in an open wound. And especially after I just told ya I still care."

"Caring isn't the same as loving, Noah. If you're not willing to be all in, I don't want to know about how you're feeling. It's not fair to me."

"Sure, and I know it. But it doesn't mean I can shut off those feelings."

Turning away, she dropped her head onto folded arms. "I must be mad, because I can't understand why you ended it to begin with."

"You work for me. I can't take advantage of the situation now, can I? What would that make me but a predator for using my position to shag ya?"

Her head came round, and she stared at him in astonishment. "You're a feckin' eejit, Noah Riley! If a woman's in love with ya and you've dated for a time, *and* she starts workin' for you, then you're not taking advantage." She jumped up and thumped him on the forehead. "Yeah, and that's closing the stall door after the fucking horse has gone! *Eejit!*"

With a deep laugh Fi felt to her toes, he pulled her down onto his lap. Her heart spasmed in her chest as she gazed into his merry eyes. Would these involuntary feelings always happen when she looked at him? She'd believed they would until the kiss with Patrick.

"Let me up, you tool."

All teasing died away, and his look was pure longing. "Will you love me forever, Fionola Bohannon?"

The desire to say yes was strong, but she held her tongue and shifted her face away to hide her weakness. Because that's what it felt like to love him. Weakness.

Standing inside the door, with his arms folded and a scowl firmly entrenched on his visage, was Patrick O'Malley. Fi's stomach flipped, and she jumped up. Why should she feel guilty? It wasn't as if he'd followed up on their earth-shattering kiss. But oh, she'd wanted him to!

"I've news," he said without preamble. "You want I should tell ya now, or wait until tomorrow when your mam and da can be present."

"Now," she croaked.

"I'll walk you home and fill you in on what I know."

"I usually drive Fi home," Noah stated.

Of course, his was a bald-faced lie. Never once had he driven her home, because they both knew damn well she teleported to save time when she was tired.

"Do ya, now?" Patrick seemed more amused than annoyed, and Fi was left to wonder if it wasn't because he recognized Noah's ploy for what it was.

"I can see myself home," she said, raising her chin in a haughty manner to show she meant business. If these two thought she'd be the rope in their ridiculous tug-of-war, they were cracked in the head.

Respect was reflected back at her from Patrick's eyes, causing Fi to release a pent-up breath.

"Unless you were raised in a barn, shut the door," Noah ordered as he rose and sauntered toward the bar. He set up three glasses for a pour and nodded toward the table. "I'd like to know what you found out, so we can discuss it here if it works for both of you."

Patrick held Fi's chair and scooted it forward as she sat down.

"Or maybe he's after keepin' an eye on the competition, yeah?" he murmured.

"Are you? The competition?" She met his steady gaze.

"Do you want me to be?"

Half of her did. The other half, the one still in love with Noah, wasn't sure she was ready for another heartbreak. Eventually, Patrick would leave. In her experience, that's what men did. She didn't have what it took to tempt a man to stay forever.

His smile was wry when he said, "I distinctly remember you saying you weren't interested."

"That was before our kiss," she retorted.

"So you've changed your mind?" The intensity in his eyes ramped up, as if he was once again a falcon watching its prey.

Noah slapped the mugs on the table with a harrumph and rescued Fi from the tractor beam caused by Patrick's hypnotic stare.

"What did you discover?" she asked after everyone was seated. "Is Tadhg all right, then?"

"I can't say with any certainty, but he was seen in Dublin just yesterday."

"Are you positive it was him?" She shared a confused look

with Noah. Her brother hated the city and avoided it at all costs.

Irritation came and went across Patrick's countenance, and his mouth firmed into a thin line. "No less than three people confirmed it, but if you want to go yourself, I'll give ya the addresses of those I spoke with."

"How did you verify it was him they saw?" Noah watched him with a thoughtful expression, as if weighing everything the man said for the truth.

"The pictures given to me." Patrick's gaze darted between the two of them before settling on her. "This is what I've been tasked to do by Anu, Fionola. If you don't trust me, then fair enough, but I'll still be on the hunt for Tadhg, all the same."

She laid her hand over his fisted one, entwining her fingers with his when he twisted his wrist and exposed his palm. "I trust you, Patrick."

"I'm after headin' back to Dublin tomorrow if you're interested in going with me."

A small thrill shot through her. Should she? Did she dare be alone with him for any length of time? What did she really know about him?

"She has a job," Noah stated flatly. "She'll stay."

His highhandedness was the determining factor.

"I'll go," she said.

"Fi." His usual seductive timbre was gone as he voiced his frustration in that one syllable.

"He's my brother, Noah, and he's hurting."

His breathing turned erratic, and a wild expression entered his eyes. "I don't like it, and I don't trust him." Noah nodded toward Patrick. "He looks at you like…" With a shake of his head, he guzzled the contents of his pint glass and slammed it on the tabletop. "Yeah, and you'll do what you want. You always do, so I'll shut my gob now. But be careful, love."

With that, he rose and stalked away, leaving Fi to stare at an empty seat as she considered what he'd said.

"You can stay if you fear me," Patrick said quietly. "I'll not take offense."

She met his compassionate gaze, and his consideration for her feelings strengthened her resolve. "When do we leave?"

An emotion remarkably similar to satisfaction flashed across his face, and a smile curled his too-tempting mouth. "I'll come for you at half past nine. That should give you plenty of time to inform your mother and father where you're going."

Fi touched his wrist and felt the zing throughout her body. After sucking in a sharp breath, she blew it out slowly.

"I feel it, too," he said in a low voice. "This thing. If it's not what you want, if who you want is him, 'tis best to stay behind and let me locate Tadhg. I'll find him and bring him home to you."

"If he's paranoid and on the run, he won't welcome your help, Patrick."

His open expression vanished, and he nodded.

Frowning, she lifted her pint and wet her dry throat. What had she said to cause him to close up tighter than a drum? She replayed their conversation in her mind and did a mental forehead slap. Her answer had sounded as if she didn't really want to be with him, but she would suffer through it for her brother's sake.

With a careful study of his face, she said, "I didn't say I wanted Noah."

"Aye, but you didn't say you didn't."

Her lips twitched. His salty expression pleased her. Maybe it was the honest emotion behind it, but he gave the impression of not liking games, and Fi couldn't be more on board with it.

"True. So let me say it straight. I'd like to go with you to find Tadhg, Patrick O'Malley. And if you'd like to request another kiss or five, I'm willing."

CHAPTER 6

$\mathcal{M}$orning came too soon and much too bright. Where was the overcast day to hide the blinding sun when Patrick needed it to temper his hangover? The last thing he remembered was picking up a bottle after a stroll in the moonlight with Fionola. He'd dropped her at her doorstep with two of those five kisses and the promise of a half-nine visit before he'd hightailed it home. Stealing the whiskey from Lucky O'Malley's storeroom was an eejit move, but he'd needed it to drown the temptation of returning to steal the other three kisses from her temptress lips.

With a groan, he rolled toward the nightstand and lifted his smartphone, promptly swearing. He'd forgotten to charge the fecking thing. If he gave it a magical boost, he risked destroying the components. After plugging it in, he staggered to the bathroom to splash frigid water on his puffy face, wincing when he met his bloodshot eyes in the mirror.

Jaysus! He looked a sight!

Then and there, he swore it was the last time he'd overindulge. Despite his troubles—and of those he had plenty—he was useless as tits on a bull after an all-nighter.

The moment the phone's battery held enough life, the chiming began, alerting him to the fact he'd missed his window to meet Fionola. She'd have his arse for certain. As he wove his way back toward the nightstand, the bedroom door flew open.

He didn't know who was more shocked, Fionola or himself.

Her eyes flared wide as she took in the *entire* package, pausing overly long to linger on his cock. Never in his life had he worried about nonsensical things like modesty, but he'd been caught in the raw, and his instinctual response was to cover the family jewels.

Slapping his hands over his junk, he scowled his ire. "What the feckin' hell do you think you're doing, bursting into a strange man's room the way ya are?" he demanded.

"I grew worried when you failed to show up. And I knocked, but you didn't answer." She'd yet to tear her curious gaze away from his nakedness, and his body's reaction, although natural, was embarrassing.

"Come in if you're so intrigued by my cock or get out. But don't stand there with the feckin' door open for all of sundry to see, yeah? I'm proud of what I own, but not that much."

She giggled. Flat out giggled like a schoolgirl peering into the boys' locker room and getting an eyeful.

"Never doubt I'm intrigued, Patrick O'Malley, but I'll be leaving you to dress, all the same." She cast his body a regretful glance and sighed. "Maybe after a time, I can get a closer look."

Fionola sailed out the door, closing it behind her. It did nothing to muffle her laughter from the other side. Funny thing about that laughter—*it triggered his.* And he flopped back on the mattress and let loose until tears were streaming from his eyes.

When he'd sobered, he brushed away the moisture alongside his temples and tried to recall when he'd last found true humor in anything. The answer was *years.* Well before Loman had imprisoned and murdered him. Farther back still, to right before he'd learned Rose was unhappy and spreading her thighs for anything with a third leg. It seemed he'd forgotten how to enjoy life. And wasn't that tragic? It boiled down to two people altering his fate, crushing his spirit, and making him miserable.

But it had taken only one person to spark a fire in him again.

Fionola Bohannon.

And though he was older than her by at least twenty years and witches like them didn't age in the way of standard mortals, Patrick felt at least five times that. But he could appreciate her natural beauty and unfailingly kind heart. Her saucy personality didn't hurt either.

As he showered and dressed, he considered distancing himself from her. Being close to her was too dangerous, making him feel and desire more than he should. She wasn't for him, and the truth of it was disheartening.

Fifteen minutes after she'd barged into his room, Patrick met Fionola downstairs in the inn's kitchen, where Bridget was cleaning up the last of the breakfast dishes.

"Why not use your shiny new magic, me love?" he asked, giving her a peck on her flawless cheek. He desperately wanted to turn back time and ruffle her brilliant ginger hair like when she'd been a small girl, but grown-up Bridget might knock him into next week.

"Habit," she said simply. "And it keeps me busy. You know I'm not one who loves to be idle, Da. It would send me round the bend."

"Aye. But you should take your young man and enjoy a day or two away. Let your good-for-nothing brothers run things for a weekend, yeah?"

"Ach! And we do our fair share," Cian protested laughingly as he rose from the table. "But it's never as good as Bridget prefers, to be sure."

"Because you're a lazy scut, Cian O'Malley." Bridget tossed a dish towel at his head. "But dry if you've a mind."

Fionola sipped tea as his family teased each other. Her expression was one of sadness, with worry creeping in along the edges.

"We'll find Tadhg," Patrick assured her.

"What's this?" Cian paused in conjuring a magical windstorm to dry dishes and returned to the table. "Who's Tadhg?"

"My brother. He's been missing for a week now." Although her voice cracked, Fionola lifted her chin, and grim determination entered her soulful eyes. "Your father has agreed to help me find him."

With a confused frown, Cian looked at him. "Da? When did you start investigating missing people? And why didn't you ask me? I've connections through the Witches' Council."

"Because the boy's running scared," Patrick snapped. "And since when do I need you to do my work for me?"

Cian stepped back and expressed shock at the vehement response. Indeed, they all appeared surprised by his surliness, Fionola included, and Patrick felt like an arse for allowing his temper to get the better of him.

"Yeah, and it's sorry I am for being a bear." Going to the medicine cabinet, he opened the door. "Bridget, me love. Where's the potion to make me right as rain?"

"I'm cooking a new batch, Da. It's cooling on the range."

After grabbing a mug from the drainboard, he spooned his granny's elixir into it and shot it straight. The taste was appalling, but the magical mixture was fast-acting and would cure what ailed him within minutes.

When he glanced up, two pairs of wary eyes watched him, as if waiting for another explosion. The only one who looked at him with understanding was Fionola, but hers was the hardest gaze to meet.

Still, he could use Cian's connections if it meant locating Tadhg faster.

"Your help would be greatly appreciated, son. If you'll sit a spell, we'll tell ya what we know."

Patrick's behavior toward his adult children was loving, if gruff, and Fi recognized he was a man used to caring for his needs last, without any assistance. Her heart ached for him. What must it be like to be your own refuge, with no true understanding of how to lean on another?

While she'd waited for him to dress, Fi conversed with Bridget and, in doing so, learned some of what Patrick had endured at Loman's hands. Of how he'd died and his Guardian daughter brought him back from the Otherworld upon her escape. Fi's brother had told her something similar.

Her chest had tightened to hear of Patrick's trials, and her reaction to his pain was stronger than any she'd felt for another not related to her. A large part of her wanted to hold him and never let go, but the realistic side of her understood he'd strongly object to anyone smothering him with caring and good intentions.

As she listened to him discuss his options with Cian, she instinctively knew he was the one destined to find Tadhg. Her knight in shining armor, as it were. When he glanced up, their gazes locked, causing her belly to flutter like mad, as if a hundred butterflies were beating against the walls of her abdomen and attempting to escape. Did he feel it, too? This bizarre connection? This drawing? For an overlong moment, his focus lingered on her mouth, but a shutter of sorts fell over him, and he looked away, almost dismissively. Almost as if he were rejecting the possibility of more.

Why?

Did he not feel deserving? Did he not believe *she* was? Old insecurities struck, and Fi sipped her tea to calm her jittery nerves, forcing her attention back to the conversation between father and son. As she listened, she compared the men. Cian bore a striking resemblance to Patrick, and there was no doubt he possessed his father's take-charge attitude. Yet only the elder O'Malley appeared resistant to anyone else's assistance. This was made plain when he grumbled about the list of Council names his son produced as potential allies in the hunt for Tadhg.

"And you think the man's in Dublin, then?" Bridget asked.

"Aye. Just days ago, he was spotted by no less than three others. My hope is he's still there." Patrick finished his drink and rose. "I'd best be going. Son, if you're able to discover Tadhg's whereabouts, text me the information, yeah?"

"Sure, and I will."

"Thanks." Shifting toward her, Patrick held out a hand. "If you're going with me, Fionola Bohannon, you'd best hold on. My teleportation skills don't work as they should these days."

"Do you have a picture of where we're going? I can use my magic to get us there."

He scrolled through his phone, and once he found what he was looking for, he handed it to her. With a nod, she wrapped an arm around his trim waist and gazed up at him. If her heart beat a little faster than it should, she ignored it.

"Ready?"

This close to him, she could see the banked fire in his eyes, and a thrill shot through her as he focused on her mouth.

"Ready," he said in his deep, reverberating voice. Or maybe it merely felt deep because his chest was pressed to hers. Either way, the sexy timbre was one her ears appreciated.

Closing her eyes, she recalled the picture he'd shown her, but as her cells began to warm, something went wrong. The image in her mind blanked, and Fi had the discombobulated sensation of tumbling through space. Her arms tightened around Patrick as she tried to recall the inn's kitchen and anchor them. But it was no use.

The homey walls of Black Cat Inn were nowhere to be seen. In their place was gray stone, and the two of them currently stood in what appeared to be the glass-and-cinder-block cell she'd seen the other day.

"Jaysus!"

CHAPTER 7

"*W*here are we?" she asked. Fi's voice was little better than a croaking toad, and to her own ears, it sounded as if it belonged to someone else.

A savage curse erupted from Patrick, and he ran for the opening, only to be met with three-inch metal bars clanking into place. She rushed to join him, unsure what she intended to do other than find a way out and back home.

"No!" As she reached for the bars, he flung out an arm and blocked her path.

"Are you mad? We have to get out of here! We have to—"

"Touch those bars, and you'll fry the skin off your feckin' arms, woman!"

He was as surly as a lion with a sore tooth, and Fi didn't blame him one bit. Between Tadhg's and Bridget's retellings, she'd been able to piece together most of Patrick's backstory. They'd explained to her how when he'd been held captive by Loman, he'd plunged his arms through the bars in an attempt to choke the fecker, only to suffer severe burns. But he hadn't let go, and his arms resembled crisp bacon strips when it was all over. The story seemed fantastical, but how else did Patrick know the bars were supercharged?

Infusing steel in her tone, she said, "Sure, and you still haven't answered me, Patrick O'Malley. *Where the feck are we?*"

For the briefest instant, his mouth curled, as if he found her humorous, but his faint smile was replaced by a grimace. Looking everywhere but at her, he shook his head.

"Patrick, please."

She hated the tremor in her voice, but her emotional state was inching toward panic. If another child disappeared on Mam and Da, they'd not recover.

"'Tis but a dream, it is," he murmured, seeming confused.

Fi touched her hand to his ice-cold cheek. "Does this not feel real to you, then?"

Under her palm, his skin heated and the confusion left him. After jerking away, he stared at her in dismay. As if waking from his supposed dream, he studied the cell with new eyes. With each passing second, his expression darkened.

"How?" he muttered. "The fucker's supposed to be dead."

"What 'fucker' are you referring to?"

Before he could respond, a hooded figure passed across the opening with their face averted.

Fi charged forward only to be halted by Patrick's arm around her waist.

"Don't!" he snapped. "Remember what I told ya, girl. The bars are electrified."

"At forty-three, I'm hardly a girl."

Yeah, she was surly, but nothing annoyed her more than being treated as an empty-headed twat. Not to mention the solid feel of his embrace was electrifying all on its own. And wasn't that scattering her wits to the wind? Or it would if there was any air blowing about. Come to think of it, why wasn't there any air? Why were her lungs unbearably tight?

She gulped in a breath.

Then another.

And another.

"Don't panic on me, love. We've enough trouble on our hands, yeah?" Patrick's soothing tone was compelling in nature and had the desired effect of calming her. "Are ya all right, now? Enough to be removing your nails from my puir, abused arm?"

With a gasp, she released him and shifted around. His mouth kicked up on the left, and his eyes dropped to her lips, then farther down to where their chests met. When he raised his gaze to hers, it glowed with an unholy light.

"You wouldn't be knowing this, love, but I've not been with a woman in some time. If you continue to press your glorious tits against me, I'm likely to embarrass us both with a cockstand."

"Be that as it may, it's difficult to move with your arm locked around my waist." Fi was proud of her level tone. Inside, her heart raced like a runaway train, and she feared he'd hear the thudding at any moment.

His arm tightened a fraction, and he once again looked at her mouth. Stark hunger shone in his face, but he nodded and released her.

She didn't immediately step away.

Instead, she lifted the hands she'd rested against his chest, running them along his collarbone and up his neck to entwine her fingers in his thick hair. She marveled at the silky texture. In her experience, gray hair tended to be courser, more wiry. His wasn't, and her growing obsession with touching it was problematic.

"What are ya doin'?"

He didn't seem displeased, merely curious, and Fi shook her head in bemusement.

What *was* she doing? They were trapped in a cage by an unknown abductor, but her body didn't get the memo. All she wanted was to explore his body. To feel his mouth on hers. To bask in the warmth emanating from him. The press of his budding erection against her abdomen woke her to the inappropriateness of her actions.

"I'm begging your pardon, Patrick."

"There's no need for that. I'd be the devil's own liar if I said I didn't enjoy it." Although his voice was gruff, his lips quirked and humor lit his emerald eyes.

They were lighter in color, and the effect was startling.

"Why are you happier here, like this, when you weren't at your home?"

All light left him, and he moved away.

"Patrick?"

"Can you believe I forgot where I was for a moment? You took me from hell to heaven, but I should've remembered that I live in a hell of my own making."

"How's that, then?"

He merely shrugged off her question and turned his broad back. "You should get comfortable, love. It's going to be a long while before anyone knows we're missing."

"DA'S GONE MISSING," Bridget informed the remaining three of her four siblings as they gathered with their mates around the table. "Cian and I were there when he began to teleport, but the room went black. Like someone turned off the lights."

Cian, the oldest of her three brothers, rose and shut the double doors leading to the pub from their private meeting room. The low light caught the strands of his dark-blond hair, causing a gleam, not dissimilar to an angel's halo, though he could be a demon spawn when riled. When he returned to his seat, his normally bright eyes were dark with concern.

"What's this, then? And how do ya know he's missing?"

Carrick's black brows clashed together in the center of his forehead. As the most serious of the O'Malleys, he always took things to heart, and the worry on his face said he'd do whatever it took to make the situation better.

Cian shrugged and answered matter-of-factly. "When I teleported directly after them, they were nowhere to be found."

"Them?"

"He's with a woman named Fionola Bohannon."

With a heartfelt sigh, Ronan rubbed the back of his neck and stared at them in confusion. "Who's she?"

"The sister of a man gone missing. Her brother's name is Tadhg Bohannon, and he was one of Loman's victims on the island," Bridget explained. "And before ya ask, she's as lovely as the day is long. She's not involved in this other than to be a victim herself. I'm sure of it."

Cian nodded. "Sure, and I agree."

"Is it possible Patrick and Fionola changed their minds and went somewhere else?" Eoin's mate, Brenna, was a shy creature and tended to stay silent unless spoken to, but in the last year, she'd grown comfortable around the O'Malleys and come out of her shell a little at a time.

"Aye, anything is possible. But he's been gone over twenty-four hours now, and tonight is Aeden's birthday celebration. Da promised to be here for it." Bridget heaved an impatient sigh and pushed her wayward auburn hair away from her forehead. Although her father's focus had been turned inward since his return from the Otherworld, the man wasn't selfish. And he certainly wouldn't miss his grandson's birthday if he could help it.

"He's been absentminded of late," Dubheasa added, stating what Bridget had just been thinking. "Could it be he's just gone off and forgotten?"

Feeling helpless, which wasn't at all like herself, Bridget simply stared at her family. What could she say? Yes, it was possible he'd lost track of time again, but how did she explain this disappearance felt different, more urgent in nature?

"Aye," she finally replied.

"But you don't believe so?" asked Piper Thorne. Her amber eyes were thoughtful as she studied Bridget, and she saw what the others didn't: Bridget's anxiety. But then, she'd always been perceptive. Likely, it came with the name Thorne. The Thorne family needed to continually be alert to danger. Theirs was a magic everyone envied and would do their best to destroy if possible. The surname brought enemies slinking out of the shadows.

A little over a year ago, the American had wandered into their pub while on vacation. With one flirty conversation, Cian had fallen head-over-heels for the dark-haired beauty, and Bridget had enjoyed watching their dance, as clumsy as it was.

"No, I don't." She sank into her chair and lifted her pint glass for a sip, needing the rich taste of Gran's brew to moisten her dry mouth. "The others were too young to remember"—with a nod, she indicated Eoin and Dubheasa—"but Da's not the same as he was. When he's not taking the piss, he's angry or dismissive."

"Sure, and I've noticed," Carrick said with a sage nod.

As the serious one of their family, he was a watcher. Similar in looks to Dubheasa, with his black hair and green eyes, he possessed a calmer temperament and tended to consider a problem from all angles before jumping in head first, as Cian and Dubheasa were wont to do.

Only Eoin, Dubheasa's twin, remained quiet on the subject, as if he didn't care about Patrick's safety one way or the other. And perhaps he didn't. Their da had disappeared when the twins were young, and Eoin had never formed a connection to him. Hell, he didn't know the man. How was he supposed to feel love for a total stranger?

Granted, Da had practically been forced from his home by

their mother and held prisoner for years by Loman O'Connor, that horrid gobshite. The youngest members of their clan, Dubheasa and Eoin had felt abandoned, though. As a moody artist, her brother internalized his feelings until he could display them on a canvas or through sculpting.

The double doors burst open, startling them all.

A tall black-haired man with midnight-colored eyes stepped through the entryway, and Bridget had the fleeting thought he, although more rugged and a helluva lot less pristine in nature, resembled the Aether with his seductive, dark looks.

"This is a private meeting," she snapped. "You'll be taking yourself back out the way you came and shutting those doors behind you, ya will."

His brows practically hit his hairline. "And you must be related to Patrick O'Malley. He's an arrogant fecker, too."

All her brothers stood. Menace was in every line of their bodies, and the fight had entered their narrowed eyes.

Bridget laughed.

Their visitor wasn't wrong. The O'Malleys were arrogant when the occasion warranted.

"What is it you're after, then?" she asked in a less combative tone.

"I'm looking for Fi. Uh, Fionola Bohannon. She's my... she..." He ran a hand through his already tussled hair and sighed. "Fi works for me, and she didn't show for her shift tonight."

"Aye. I'm not surprised. She was with my Da, and they've not returned from Dublin." Bridget gestured for him to join them. "Close the doors."

Once he was seated with his back to a wall, the man sent each of them an assessing glance, summing them up in an instant. She was curious what opinion he'd formed, but she wouldn't ask.

"Are ya planning on introducing yourself anytime soon?" Eoin asked.

"I'm Noah Riley. I own The Jaded Nomad down Wexford way."

"I've visited your place," Cian replied as he leaned back and hooked an arm over the top of his chair. "Seems a long way to come in search of a missing server."

Noah's mouth tightened. "Fi's more than that."

"Does she know it?" her brother asked with a disbelieving laugh. "She was mighty friendly with our Da."

"She knows."

But his expression said he wasn't as sure as he pretended.

CHAPTER 8

$\mathcal{F}$ ionola curled into the warm body next to her and sighed as she fought wakefulness. She hadn't forgotten where she was, but Patrick's large frame and protective arms made her feel safe throughout the long hours of the night when she woke disoriented and afraid.

Over the last thirty-six hours, the hooded figure had ignored their attempts to get his or her attention. Food appeared whenever they weren't paying attention or while they were sleeping, frustrating Fi to no end. If only they could catch the person in the act, they might get answers.

Patrick had acclimated quickly, as if being in a cage didn't bother him in the least. Yet there were times when his lips would thin and a white line of tension appeared around his mouth. Sweat would bead his brow, and he seemed to appreciate when she'd soothe him with a simple touch.

"Tell me this is all a dream," she murmured as she snuggled into him. "Tell me we're not trapped in a cage for Goddess knows how long until someone realizes we're missing."

"I wish I could, love." His voice was raspy and strained, causing her to shift and study his expression. Fatigue lined his face, and worry tugged at his brow. In his eyes, she could see pain, but she didn't know if it was physical or emotional, considering his history with incarceration.

"Are you all right, Patrick? Truly?"

"Aye."

She sensed the lie, but if he didn't want to discuss it, what was she to do? Rolling to a sitting position, she stretched her arms over her head and moved her neck from side to side. The gestures were more out of habit than any need for bodily relief. The bed was oddly comfortable for a prison cell, but she didn't want to question it.

"Why haven't they begun to drain our magic?" she asked in a hushed voice. "Isn't that what was done to you and Tadhg when you were last here?"

Patrick shifted to lie flat on his back and stare up at the ceiling. He remained quiet for such an inordinate amount of time that she assumed he wouldn't answer. There were instances over the last day and a half when he'd ignored her endless questions, and she figured this might be one of them.

With a heavy sigh, he turned his head and met her curious gaze. "Aye. It's what they did. These cells were designed to drain witches a bit at a time. But Loman O'Connor grew bolder, and whoever was unfortunate enough to find themselves a guest of his was eventually bled dry of their magic. Sometimes their life force, too."

Hatred, burning and fierce, blazed in his expressive eyes. Before yesterday, she'd have said Patrick kept his cards close to his chest. Yet little by little, since they'd found themselves the unwilling guests of a maniac, he opened up, allowing her to see below his crusty exterior to the soft center. Whenever their food arrived, he allowed her to have the choice bits and to eat her fill, before consuming what was left. He'd also constructed a screen for the toilet area from a sheet, and he was courteous when she needed privacy, turning his back and humming so she wasn't embarrassed by the forced intimacy.

"Your stay here had to be horrendous for you," she said softly.

"Aye. But it was worse for those who didn't survive."

He rolled to his feet and rubbed the back of his neck, before hung his head for a long minute. Unable to ignore his internal pain, she stroked his back and rested her cheek against his shoulder.

"I'm sorry."

"None of it was your fault, love. 'Tis sorry I am you were dragged into my mess this time around."

"You're not to blame for any of this, Patrick. You were trying to help me find Tadhg."

He avoided her gaze as he rose and crossed to their breakfast tray. "If not me, who?"

"Whoever's behind our abduction!" Fi leapt to her feet and wormed her way between him and the wall, forcing him to look at her. "You're blameless. You have to know that."

His expression was tortured, and she did the only thing she knew how to do. She wrapped her arms around his neck and tucked his face against her throat as she stroked his thick hair.

"You're blameless," she reiterated, dropping a light kiss on the shell of his ear.

His steely arms encircled her, and he held her so tightly to him that she worried for her ribs. But the feel of her sensitive breasts against his hard, muscle-defined chest felt too good for her to argue about his crushing embrace.

"Your heart is pure, Fionola Bohannon," he said in a voice bordering tender. His lips brushed her throat, and she shivered at the electrical sensation the contact caused. Heat pooled low in her abdomen, and despite the fact they were prisoners, she experienced a rightness. As if being here, with him, was where she was supposed to be.

"I'm not pure of heart. Far from it," she admitted. "I've a fierce temper, and I've been known to have horrid thoughts about others, though I've not voiced more than ten percent of them."

His chuckle curled her toes and sent a tingle up her legs.

"Then you're the perfect woman." He drew back and stared down at her for the longest time. His voice was hoarse when he finally said, "So fucking beautiful, ya are."

The urge to kiss him was stronger than any she'd had, but she simply stroked his stubbled cheek. "I'm not winning any contests, that's for damned sure. But I appreciate you think I could, all the same."

His thumb swept across her lower lip in a gentle caress. One that was so simple, yet seductive, Fi had a hard time not panting her sudden aching need. For levity, she bit the pad of his thumb.

"I'm after eating breakfast. It's been too long between meals, I'm thinking."

She wasn't positive, but she thought she heard him mutter, "I'm after eating something much more tasty," as she stepped away. Spinning back, she asked, "What did you say?"

He grinned but remained mute.

Fi wagged her finger at him. "Behave. It's not the time nor place for such foolishness."

All teasing left him, and he nodded sharply. "Aye."

As Patrick watched Fionola consume her portion of their breakfast, he pondered her question from earlier. Why *hadn't* their magic been syphoned? Who was behind this fiasco, and why were they holding back? For that matter, why hide their identity behind shadows and hoods? What did it gain them?

By now, Cian and Bridget would realize he was in trouble, as Noah no doubt did when Fi failed to show for work. It wouldn't be long before they consulted with others in an attempt to locate them. Patrick only had to keep her safe until they were found.

He meandered toward the bars, angling to look down the hall. No windows were visible, and any light along the corridor appeared to be artificial in nature. The air was controlled and neither too hot nor too cold. The place was the same, as was the cell placement, but the lack of sound disturbed him, and it was vastly different from his incarceration before. He'd never say it aloud, though. If Fionola hadn't registered their total isolation yet, he didn't want to add to her worry.

"Do you think Tadhg's here?"

He glanced over his shoulder to find her watching him. The fierce intensity on her lovely face was an indication of her unspoken worry. He wouldn't lie if asked directly, though he preferred not to volunteer information if he could avoid it. She was clever and would figure the inconsistencies out for herself in due time.

"Aye. Among others."

"The previous victims who went missing?"

He nodded and turned back toward the bars. In the distance, a shadow shifted, and Patrick leaned forward to see better. He'd failed to properly calculate the distance to the bars, and he hissed out a breath when his skin connected with the supercharged metal.

Fionola cried out and rushed to him, fingers outstretched to touch the burn. Whether to heal or explore the scorched skin, he didn't know, but he ducked away to avoid contact.

Confusion reflected back from her lovely eyes as they danced across his burned skin. "There's no mark," she exclaimed. "Shouldn't it be red at least?"

Not red? It throbbed like the dickens. How was it not marked? He touched his cheekbone and winced from the pain.

"Is your vision bad, then?" he asked.

"My vision is fine, thank you very much!"

Her salty response teased a smile from his lips. What did it say about him that he liked her sassiness? When pink colored Fionola's cheeks, Patrick realized he'd stared too long. Heat crept up his neck, and he opened his mouth to apologize. Anything he might've said was cut off as the cloaked figure swept by the doorway.

As Fionola unthinkingly grabbed for the bars, Patrick wrapped an arm around her waist and swung her away. Pressing her to the wall, he gripped her wrists and frantically searched for burns, sighing his relief when she appeared to be unharmed.

"Jaysus! Never do that again, woman! You could've been electrocuted."

Her wide-eyed stare held wariness and caused his stomach to tighten.

His anger probably seemed unjustified to her, but for him, the image of her blistered skin churned his guts and made him want to vomit. Hell, the idea of her hurt at all shriveled his bollocks, and that realization had him releasing her faster than if he'd held a sizzling pan without a potholder. He'd no need of caring and relationships other than what he already had with his children. Falling for Fionola Bohannon was a recipe for disaster.

She was already in love with another.

CHAPTER 9

Noah paced the confines of the Black Cat Inn's parlor, sick with worry for Fi. Another night had passed with no sign of her, and he was ready to lose his bloody mind. The O'Malley's had used their full range of resources, to no avail.

Why had he let her go? His instincts had argued against it, against allowing her to run off with a stranger, regardless of the fact she wasn't Noah's to protect. But he'd wanted to be. Why had he let his past color his future? Why not go all in when he'd had the chance?

He was a bloody fool, was why.

"We should contact the Aether," Ronan said grimly.

Noah paused in his pacing.

The Aether.

The one person he never wanted to meet.

"Are you all right there, Noah?" Cian asked. The other man's watchfulness was natural for someone who'd worked for the Witches' Council, as Cian had. As a spy, he would've learned to study movement and expression. Noah imagined it came in handy for him in situations such as these.

"Aye," he lied. "I'm worried about Fi, and the not knowing is distressing."

"Understandable." But there was doubt in Cian's keen-eyed stare. "Have you met the Aether, then?"

It took all of his willpower not to react to the name. This time, he didn't need to lie. "No."

"What do you have against him?"

"Who said I did?" he snapped, immediately giving himself away. "For feck's sake, it's no one's business, yeah? I don't know the man, and that should be enough."

Ronan approached him, and the Guardian's power flared to life, blinding him and forcing him to throw up his hands to shield his eyes.

Fucker could tone it down!

"I could, but then you wouldn't have given me the response I was after, would you?" Ronan replied aloud.

Dropping his arms, Noah locked gazes with him.

"You can read my mind?" he asked silently.

"No. But it seems you can telegraph what it is you're wanting others to know." A wary look settled on Ronan's face, and his silvery eyes narrowed with displeasure. "Who and *what* are you?"

"I'm a pub owner. That's all. I've no special abilities other than those of a standard witch."

"Somehow I doubt that," replied a cultured voice from behind him.

Noah's arsehole clenched.

The voice was similar to the one from his childhood. The one he'd grown up answering to whenever he stepped out of line. That of his father, Damarius Dethridge. But it couldn't be Da. He was long dead.

Gathering his courage, Noah turned.

The black-haired man bore no resemblance to his father, just as Noah hadn't. Damarius had been golden with blue eyes leaning toward gray. They'd darkened in later years, becoming the color of a storm cloud, and eventually they turned flat, as if the weight of his sadness had stolen all the light from his soul. Other than his handsomeness, there wasn't much to recommend his father. No shining personality traits that made him stand out amongst the crowd.

But then again, he'd lost his wife and young son to the Darkness, an evil far greater than any could imagine. Damarius had barely escaped into the night with baby Noah bundled tightly in his arms, and he'd mourned for his remaining days. As did Noah, for a mother and big brother who would never be his. For a childhood that should've been filled with love and laughter, but was instead void of both.

The Aether was an inch or two shorter than Noah's six-feet-one, but his presence commanded attention. While the man wasn't slight in stature, he wasn't bulky either. Indeed, his build was somewhere in between, suggesting he was lean and fit underneath his elegant shirt and slacks. His obsidian-colored irises were dark enough to make them blend with his pupils if it hadn't been for the silver slivers. The surprise in them was amusing if one were inclined to think shocking an Aether was a good thing.

"Hello, big brother," Noah said. "I'm guessing by your surprise, you didn't know I existed, yeah?"

One or two of the others present gasped, and behind him Bridget crowed, "Pay up, ya scut! Sure, and didn't I tell ya they were related?"

But he ignored them as he watched the range of emotions—disbelief, acceptance, regret, along with a host of others not so easily discernible—flit across the perfectly symmetrical face of his only sibling.

"How?" Damian Dethridge slowly approached him, and his practiced casualness would be off-putting to someone who didn't recognize it covered deeper feelings. Noah had utilized the trick himself on many occasions.

"Are you asking *how* I exist? The normal way, I'm guessing." Yes, he was being flippant, but old habits died hard, and the smooth voice was too similar to their father's, grating on his last nerve. Although a muscle twitched along his brother's sculpted jaw, any other sign of his irritation wasn't visible to the others.

Noah felt it, though.

He hadn't lied to Ronan in that he didn't possess many abilities, but the ones he did were those of an empath and a telepath, along with the standard witchy gifts of teleportation and conjuring what he needed. All the extras he'd been born with were bound by his father and a Goddess known to his da. By using a two-superior-being whammy to remove what should've been Noah's, Damarius had ensured those abilities would stay bound long after his death.

"I didn't know about your existence," Damian said smoothly, recovering well. "How is it you've been able to stay hidden as long as you have?"

"Sure, and that would be goddess magic."

"Which one?" Although the cadence of the Aether's tone was even, his emotions beneath the surface were a bubbling cauldron and would require nothing to boil over.

Noah suspected the next words he uttered might make that happen. He paused overly long and studied his brother, noting all the similarities in their appearance. Many who'd met them both had commented on the resemblance, but Noah had been quick to laugh it off with a quip or two. Acknowledging their connection was dangerous to his continued safety.

"Which one, Mr. Riley? Or should I say, *Mr. Dethridge?*" Damian asked silkily, almond-shaped eyes narrowing in warning.

It was Noah's turn to be surprised. Exactly how his brother knew his chosen name was in question.

"Ronan called me yesterday when you first arrived." The Aether plucked the thought from Noah's brain, and the smugness of his answer nearly drove Noah mad. Damian's dark eyes narrowed briefly before shooting to Ronan. "He failed to mention we look enough alike to be twins."

"Ah! That explains it, then," Noah said casually, mentally shaking off the feeling of having his mind violated. Yeah, that's what he'd done to Ronan earlier, but he figured the arrogant bastard needed to be taken down a notch.

As did the one in front of him.

"Indeed," Damian said. His expression hardened. "Now, please answer my question. Who was the Goddess?"

"Isis."

The Aether's slap of pained disbelief caused the occupants of the room to suck in their breaths or gasp at the stinging sensation.

"Dethridge! Pull it back!" Ronan barked.

With a shake of his head, Damian inhaled deeply, smoothing the look of betrayal from his face. "Did you know about me, Noah?"

"Aye."

All expression disappeared and was replaced by a mask of cool indifference—another look Noah had perfected for himself. For the longest moment, he held his breath, awaiting Damian's backlash.

It didn't come.

Their father would't have been as controlled.

"I have a lot of questions, if you care to answer them one day, but that's not why we're here, is it?" With a nod of politeness, Damian turned, his back arrow straight, and strode to Bridget. Taking her hand in his, he brought it to his lips and bussed her knuckles like a gentleman of old.

Of course, that's what they were. At over two hundred years old, Damian and Noah were of another time, when courtly manners meant something. His older brother had retained all the niceties, where Noah had done away with them over the years, adapting when necessary to fit in with the common folk. He'd designed his pub to cater to both the magical and non-magical communities, with a stern warning to witches and warlocks that no abilities were allowed in his place while those without were present.

"Ronan explained about Patrick's disappearance, my dear. I'll do what I can to help," Damian said.

"O'Malley isn't the only one missing." Anger bubbled inside Noah. It seemed everyone was so concerned with Patrick that they'd forgotten Fi and her brother were unaccounted for. "My... uh, Fionola Bohannon disappeared with him."

Assessing eyes watched him, and Noah struggled to keep his feelings hidden. He'd mistakenly revealed them to the O'Malley family, and although he had no reason to suspect Damian would hurt Fi, he didn't trust him. The grapevine had produced glowing reports about the Aether and how fair he was in his dealings, but Noah knew better and wouldn't give him the ammunition. His father had drummed into him that the Darkness lurked within their line, insisting one day Damian would accept the call of its evil, and if not him, then Noah surely would.

"Bohannon." Damian frowned and glanced at Dubheasa. "Isn't that one of the names on our list of Loman's victims?"

She nodded. "It is."

"Tadhg Bohannon is Fi's brother," Noah replied. "He's not been the same since he returned from that bleeding island."

"And he's one of many who have up and disappeared over the last year, with no word to family or friends," Ronan added grimly. "Seems someone's decided to finish what my father started."

"Have no fear, my friend. They won't succeed," Damian promised.

Through his gift, Noah sensed his brother's sincerity, and it was surprising. By nature, the Aether was an unfeeling bastard, taking magic when it suited and doling out judgments as if his own actions weren't questionable in nature.

"You're angry with me," Damian said to him abruptly. "Before we proceed, I'd like to know why."

"It's none of your feckin' business," Noah growled. "And if all anyone here plans to do is stand around, then I'll find them myself."

The suddenness of Damian's grin was disarming. "You're in love with the girl."

"I'm not!" he denied hotly. Only *he* had to know it was a lie. "And I'll have words with any who say otherwise."

Damian's black brows shot up.

"Fi works for me, and I've promised her mam and da I'd find her."

"Then find her, we shall. I—*dammit, Beastie!*"

In a flash of golden light, a young girl stood in front of Noah with a wide grin on her adorable elfin face. "Hello, Uncle Noah."

CHAPTER 10

After Patrick released her, Fi remained leaning against the wall, out of breath from the suddenness of his reaction. He'd saved her from a severe burn at the very least and possibly a heart-stopping electrical shock at the worst. His anger was born of fear, and she recognized some men reacted strongly in a situation such as theirs.

Was she afraid of him? *No.* To date, he'd been like a crusty old dog, all bark and no bite, but time would tell if he was as docile as he appeared. She suspected he wasn't. When the moment came to confront their enemy, Patrick O'Malley would seek to destroy him or her. No questions asked.

A shiver of appreciation traveled Fi's spine. Who wouldn't prize a male like him? She certainly did. "I'm sorry, Patrick. I wasn't thinking when I saw our captor walk by, and I was seeking answers."

His back tensed an instant before his shoulders dropped. When he faced her, he was contrite. "I'm sorry I manhandled you, Fionola. 'Twas purely fear driven."

"I know. I'm not angry."

The tightness left his features, and a small smile curled his engaging mouth. "Aye, and that's a good thing. There's nowhere for me to run, and I've a mighty respect for a furious woman, I do."

A laugh bubbled up, and she shook her head at his silliness.

"I've the feeling you could coax the birds from the sky, Patrick O'Malley."

His smile didn't falter, but an underlying sadness lingered in his eyes.

She clasped his wrist. "What did I say that was wrong?"

"Nothing."

"You told me you wouldn't lie when it came to Tadhg. I'm asking you now, please don't lie to me about anything else. I can't abide a liar."

He gave a single sharp nod and strolled to the breakfast tray, prepared to pick through what she'd left untouched. Fi knew he'd been allowing her to have her fill of the tastiest bites, but she was also aware his body required more calories than hers. For that reason, she'd curbed her desire to stress eat, leaving him enough to maintain his strength.

She frowned as she contemplated the arrival and disappearance of the tray. It always manifested while *she* was sleeping, but she hadn't thought to ask Patrick if he was awake for each magical delivery.

She voiced her question.

It struck her as strange when he did no more than shrug his answer.

Things weren't adding up.

"So you've been awake when the food comes?" she demanded, unwilling to let him blow it off. Somewhere inside, she knew the answer was important, but she couldn't quite figure out why. Once she had all the facts, the puzzle pieces might fall into place.

"What's it matter if I'm asleep or not? It's not as if I can make it to the door before they leave."

He sounded surly, as if he were upset she'd even mentioned it.

"Who delivers it? Is it always the same person?" And wasn't it queer that she'd been asleep every time? Breakfast, lunch, *and* dinner. What were the odds? Was she being drugged? And why only her? Why not Patrick?

"I can't see their face, so how am I supposed to know if it's the same person?" His scowl would scare another, but she was learning his moods, and his said he was being evasive.

Fi charged across the room and knocked the croissant from his hand. For a second, she was distracted by the quality of their fare. Why were prisoners receiving delicious meals? Shouldn't they be tortured with gruel and left with scummy water?

"Not two minutes ago, you agreed not to lie to me, Patrick O'Malley."

"I didn't lie."

"You're not telling the truth, though, are ya?" she snapped.

"If I'd known you were a harpy, I'd have left you behind," he snapped back.

They were toe-to-toe and nose to nose, and neither was prepared to budge on the subject.

Fi jutted up her chin. "You promised."

"That word never left my lips, woman. Not once. Promises are for fools, because life is ever-changing, and at any moment, they can be broken."

"Are you talking about our situation or your own?" she taunted. "I'm not your faithless wife, and I'd appreciate it if you didn't treat me like I was."

"No, but you're Noah's faithless girl, yeah?"

His comeback stung. "I don't belong to Noah. I don't belong to *any* man. Nor will I," she said stiffly. "And I've never been faithless. I've been the one cheated on and left behind. The one made to feel worthless."

Patrick's eyes grew dark with remorse. "I'm sorry—"

"No. You don't get to say hurtful things and then apologize like you didn't mean it. Your intent was to wound and get me to back off." Proud of her even tone, she lifted her chin and glared. "I won't. We need to work together to solve the mystery of who abducted us. They've the key to Tadhg's location, too. I'm certain of it."

"If there was anything to tell you, I would," he said by way of a peace offering.

"Yeah, and that remains to be seen," she muttered. Stomping away, she flopped on the mattress and focused on the dull gray ceiling. If she didn't get out of here soon, she'd go mad. Fi was the sort who needed to keep busy, and without any way to do that, she was bound to lose her temper, too.

"Whenever the food is delivered, I've been holding you," Patrick confessed as he approached the bed. "Our jailor has been long gone before I can untangle myself."

She turned her attention on him, but remained silent.

"You're a bleeding octopus in your sleep, ya are," he teased. With a gentle nudge of her hip, he sat down and lifted her hand to toy with her fingers. "I find myself always having to apologize to you, Fionola. And it's not what I'm used to. I've been alone a great many years and imprisoned by Loman twice in all that time."

Fi curled on her side and propped her head on her free hand, doing nothing to draw away as he continued to touch her.

"I don't know how to be human most days," he said with a rough sigh.

"Why the dig about Noah?"

"I've a hard time trusting women." Patrick shrugged and met her steady gaze. "But I want to trust you. I'm not sure how, though."

"You can trust that there's nothing between Noah and me."

His struggle against skepticism was visible in his unhappy frown, but he didn't argue.

She closed her fingers over his. "Noah ended our relationship when I began working for him. He has some outdated notion about protecting his reputation and doesn't want anyone to believe he's taking advantage of an employee."

"He's a fool."

"I'll not argue the point," she said dryly. "But he's moved on."

Patrick's green eyes sharpened. "And you, love? Have you moved on?"

"If you're asking if I care about him, the answer is yes. If you're asking if I'm waiting on him for marriage and weens, the answer is no. He made his choice."

After another long moment spent watching her, Patrick slowly nodded. "What if he came to you and told you he regretted his hasty decision?"

"He said something similar right before you arrived with news of Tadhg." Fi grimaced. "Is it wrong to want to be someone's first choice, Patrick? To not be an afterthought or a gut reaction to jealousy?"

"No. I don't believe it is," he replied in a compassionate tone. "But then again, I don't know what being first feels like. I've never been anyone's priority."

Her heart ached for them both. They were two peas in the proverbial pod.

"I'd put you first," she said, and it felt like a promise of sorts. Especially when he caressed her cheek and graced her with a smile sweet enough to make her teeth ache.

"Any man who doesn't put you first is a fucking eejit, Fionola Bohannon."

The sudden onslaught of tears stung, and she blinked rapidly to dispel them. She was unprepared when he hauled her into his arms, providing her with the comfort she wasn't aware she needed. A sob escaped, and in the next instant, they were lying on the bed with her face buried against his throat as she cried out years of heartache. Not just because of Noah's defection, but all the ones before.

"It's all right, love. Sure, and I've got you now," he assured her as he rubbed circles over her back and cradled her close. "I've got ya, Fi."

Despite being imprisoned with little hope of escape, she felt the safest she had in a long while. Patrick's strong arms were the haven she'd always longed for. Once, she believed Noah would be her North Star, but she'd been wrong.

"I was thoroughly destroyed when my wife cheated on me the first time," he told her. "The first blow's the worst when you don't see it coming. The second is a wee bit easier to suffer, and by the third, you're calling yourself all kinds of fool and blaming yourself for staying."

Fi's arms tightened in response.

"In the end, she betrayed our entire family for Loman O'Connor. Sure, and it would be difficult to find a man more evil than him." He sighed heavily. "He'd parade her in front of my cell—this exact one—showing off the bruises on her face and neck. And bugger it all if she didn't stay with him, suffering through the beatings. I'll never understand it."

"Oh, Patrick! That had to be difficult, especially loving her the way you did."

"I didn't," he said roughly. "Not since before Carrick was born. I stayed for my children. But I was faithful to her, a woman I could hardly tolerate."

Fi recalled Eoin and Dubheasa. "One assumes the passion was still alive, if you fathered the twins after."

"When you refuse to step outside your marriage, the alcohol is plentiful, and a spouse is willing, there are a few gratifying moments to be had," he said dryly.

With a snort, Fi released him. "You're to be admired for holding to your vows."

"Or pitied for the feckin' eejit I was."

"No." She cradled his face between her palms. "Don't do that, Patrick. Don't belittle your selfless act. Another would've been gone the first time."

"Aye, and likely I should've been, but I'd only to look into Bridget's fearful eyes to know leaving her with Rose wasn't an option. Protecting her and her brothers from my wife's wicked temper was paramount."

"Why didn't you kick her out?"

"By the time we all finally saw her for what she was, she was pregnant with Dubheasa and Eoin. I couldn't."

Fi didn't want to be the one to bring it up, but she had to ask. "Do you ever wonder if the twins are yours?"

"No. Their eyes are the same as mine. Few possess such a color green as the O'Malleys."

"I'm sorry."

"For asking? Don't be. It's a question many would ask if bold enough." He huffed out a laugh. "I appreciate your boldness, love."

She wanted to show him just how bold she could be, but they were in a cell under the watchful eye of their jailor, and the timing was shite.

CHAPTER 11

*N*oah was flabbergasted.

The dark-haired sprite was the spitting image of his brother in child form. But where Damian was reserved, this girl was anything but, and her engaging grin was difficult to dismiss.

Uncle Noah.

He'd had no idea she even existed, and the urge to question if Damian had more children was plaguing him. But he wouldn't because he wanted nothing to do with the Aether or the Dethridge legacy.

"I have a brother, too," the girl said. "But you're not evil, Uncle Noah. Neither is Papa. Grandpa Damarius was wrong."

Her words were a knife to his fecking heart. How did she know? And how many times had he wanted his father to see the good in him? Wanted a portion of the love the man held for Damian? There were many occasions when Noah had stumbled upon his father, drink in hand and staring at a portrait of himself with his wife and firstborn. The longing in his eyes had made Noah's stomach tighten and his heart ache. He'd only required a small token of his father's affection, and yet, he'd never received it or a kind word of any sort. More often than not, it was a boot to his backside that his father provided.

Paralyzed and helpless from the wall of emotions crashing over him, Noah was unable to answer the girl. Her obsidian eyes turned to large pools of sadness the longer she watched him, and his desire to squat down to hug her was strong. But he'd learned early to hold back or face his father's wrath, and that lesson didn't simply disappear.

"I'm Sabrina, but you can call me Beastie, like Papa," she said, holding out her hand for him to shake, clearly undeterred by his reticence.

Sabrina. A beautiful name for so lovely a child. It fit her, though he suspected Beastie was more appropriate.

He cleared his throat and took her tiny hand in his. "Noah Riley."

"I know. I'm an Oracle." She wasn't smug or arrogant, simply stating a fact, and Noah found his lips curling in response.

"That's a tough job for one so young."

"I can handle it. Papa is teaching me how to be a good Aether. I'm supposed to weigh everything I see and make an informed decision." She glanced at her exasperated father. "Isn't that right, Papa?"

"Yes. However, I also advised you to use caution, and you've ignored that important rule," Damian replied dryly.

A small kernel of something resembling respect popped within Noah as he watched father interact with daughter. Damian's parenting skills appeared to be vastly different from their da's.

"Uncle Noah needs us, Papa," she said simply. "He's been alone too long."

Another pang struck Noah's heart, but rather than embrace her as he wanted, he withdrew his hand.

"By choice," he told her with a tight smile. "You'll find when you live as long as your father and me, putting up walls is necessary."

Gah! That little tidbit had slipped out, revealing vulnerability to his potential enemy—his brother.

"I'm not your enemy, Noah," Damian said. "You'll discover I can be a great friend if you let me."

"I've enough friends, thanks." But he avoided his brother's considering gaze.

"Don't worry. He'll come around, Papa." Sabrina grinned up at him and clasped his hand again. "You just need love, Uncle Noah. We have plenty of that in our home."

"I live in Ireland, girl. Yeah, and I've no need to visit your home."

Although his voice was gruff, it didn't faze her, and she tightened her hand. What had she seen for him? He curbed the desire to ask. But if she was truly an Oracle, he had no problem seeking answers about Fi.

"Do you know where my girlfriend is, ya wee Beastie?"

She laughed.

Frowning, Noah checked the others' responses before looking down at her. "Sure, and what's the craic?"

"You called me 'wee Beastie' just like Ronan. He's a special Guardian for Baby Nate and me."

"And what am I? Chopped liver?" Dubheasa asked with a laughing glance toward her mate.

"What can I say, Dove? The wee Beastie loves me best," Ronan quipped.

"Pfft."

Noah had been around many who displayed close familial ties and friendships, but other than Fi, he'd not experienced a true connection. He'd been a fool to ignore what she'd offered, and all because he'd been terrified she was the one person who could break down his protective walls.

Yet standing in front of him, refusing to let go of him, was another pint-sized female with a similar openness, taking a battering ram to those same walls. Both were making progress in their demolition efforts.

"Fi isn't your girlfriend, Uncle Noah."

"I won't quibble over semantics," he said with a half shrug, wishing he could punch himself in the face for letting everyone know how he felt about Fi. Taking the proverbial bull by the horns, he added, "She will be when I find her again, all the same."

The extremely skeptical look from a child, like the one Sabrina was gracing him with, was disturbing. No one wanted to be called out on their shite.

"Fine. What is it you think ya know, wee Beastie?" he growled.

She cast her father a sly glance before shrugging. "I'm not allowed to tell."

Damian laughed, damn him!

"And here I was beginning to like ya," Noah muttered.

Sabrina's tinkling laughter was as pure as church bells and highly contagious, though he refused to give into it.

No one else had the same problem.

***

PATRICK AND FI spent the rest of the day together, sharing the highlights from their lives. Their stories were outrageous and the laughter plentiful, despite the situation. She silently admired his casual pose, with one leg outstretched and a sinewy forearm draped over the raised knee of the other. His eyes leaned more toward emerald today, and Fi could only assume his mood wasn't as dark as when he'd shown up on her doorstep. It could be argued he'd found meeting her family less preferable to incarceration, but she wouldn't go there.

When he bit into an apple with his straight white teeth, the juice settled on his lower lip, begging her to lean forward and lick it off. She checked the urge and glanced down at their lunch. Once again, it had appeared when she was dozing, and she could only assume there was a camera in the room, monitoring their movements, although she could detect no sign of it.

"Tell me about your parents," he encouraged. "Why does your dad drink so much?"

"We're Irish, or have you forgotten?"

He grinned. "Sure, and we all love a pint or two, but your da was well into his cups."

Fi sighed. "We lost my little brother, Jimmy, when he was just ten. It made Mam overprotective and Da an alcoholic."

"I'm sorry, love."

The truth was, although all witches possessed abilities and, to some extent, healing magic, the Goddess had her reasons for taking a soul early. Of course, the Bohannons hadn't been privy to that reason, and they missed young Jimmy something fierce.

"It's why I'm determined to escape here and find Tadhg," she told him. "They deserve better than to lose any more children."

Patrick's expression bordered on tender. "You'll make good your escape."

"It's difficult to do when the bars will cook our arses if touched." She sighed her frustration. "If only we could get an idea of who's behind this, we could formulate a plan."

With a frown and a considering glance around the room, he stood. He approached the cell door, stopping a few feet away, then tossed the apple core against the bars. Although the air around them sizzled and snapped, the fruit remains were intact with no charring or marks of any kind.

"Does that seem strange to you?" she asked when his frown darkened.

"Aye. We should be smelling something akin to burnt apple right about now."

He returned and selected a fork, then repeated the process of throwing an object at the metal bars. Once again, the atmosphere around them sizzled and snapped. This time a shimmer of green ran the length of the room from floor to ceiling.

"What the fuck?" Fi cried. "Was it like this the first time?"

"None of the times," he replied with a thoughtful scowl. "I'm going to touch the bars, and I'll be obliged to you if you heal any burns."

"Patrick, no!" She jumped up and grabbed his forearm as he stretched forward. "We haven't tried using our magic yet." Yeah, and it made no sense why they hadn't. Were they under a magical suggestion not to? An idea struck her. "Let's conjure items or try to teleport first. If either works, we can formulate a plan from there."

With a single nod, he said, "Call up a pint. I could use the drink."

She grinned and held up her hands, palms facing upward. Closing her eyes, she envisioned the glass forming, and warmth danced along her skin. The weight of the mug was heavy and grew heavier still when she imagined it filled with beer.

"Fuck me, it worked." Patrick sounded bewildered, as if he'd expected it not to. He accepted the pint and promptly shouted his surprise when the glass shattered and the liquid soaked him.

"What the hell happened? Did you intentionally break it, then?" she asked with an edge to her tone. Her frustration was great.

"Do you think I want to be soaked to the bone and reeking of beer?" he growled back.

"You try to conjure one," she demanded.

He did with the same result, ending up twice as wet as he'd started.

Fi shook her head, baffled by the entire situation. "How can we conjure something, but it goes bust the moment we do?"

"It's a feckin' mystery, it is." And he didn't sound thrilled to solve it.

CHAPTER 12

For the rest of the afternoon and into the early evening, Patrick and Fionola conjured items, only to have them explode the moment the object was completely formed. Their bodies were covered in food and drink, and it had become a game of sorts to coat the other in the messiest goo imaginable. By the time they were done, their cell looked like a war zone.

Patrick approached Fi, intent on removing the cherry pie filling from the tip of her nose, when the glob dripped onto her breast. In his mind, he envisioned her sans clothing with the rich ruby-red juice trickling along her creamy skin to a pert, dusty-rose nipple, and he'd never imagined such an alluring mess in his life.

"Do you think if we magically clean the room, the walls might explode and release us?" she teased, distracting him from his fantasy.

Thankfully!

"Aye. They'll be picking up our body parts all the way across the channel."

She laughed up at him, and he wanted to kiss her so badly

his heart ached from the longing. When her gaze dropped to his mouth, he had the stray hope that perhaps she felt their connection to the extent he did.

Swiping a finger along her cheek, he removed a glob of chocolate syrup, sniffed it, and then tasted it with a soft moan of appreciation. "It was a grand idea you had to conjure Belgian chocolate, love, but it's a bloody shame to be wasting it."

She stepped closer and repeated the gesture, grinning widely around her finger as the flavor profile struck her taste buds. Her sparkling eyes spoke to his soul, calling him to action. Bending his head, he waited a few heartbeats for her approval, and once he'd received it, he covered her mouth with his. The deliciousness of chocolate and cherries combined tempted him to delve deeper, and he swept his tongue along hers, groaning when the subtle notes of the food burst to life and satiated his senses.

Her hands traveled up his chest, explored the breadth of his shoulders, then made the journey along his neck. As her fingers dug into his hair, Patrick sighed his pleasure and went back for a second taste. His arms banded around her, and his palms itched to cup her breasts, but he gave her the lead. Whatever Fi wanted, he'd abide by. He only hoped it was a satisfying shag.

Meeting his hungry gaze, she took one of his hands in hers and placed it on her breast. "Touch me," she urged.

"It would be my greatest pleasure, love." Trailing his fingertips over the slope of her breast, he skimmed along the shape of her, then lifted the hem of her shirt for contact with her silky smooth skin.

She sucked in a breath as he ran his flat palm along her stomach and along her upper back to unclasp her bra. When she was free of constraint, Patrick cupped her bared breast and sighed his happiness as he brushed a thumb across her erect nipple.

"You're beautifully built, Fionola. It's like you were hand-crafted just for me."

She shivered and pressed into him, dropping her hands to his trouser fastening. Making short work of the button and zipper, she slid her hand beneath the waistband of his boxer briefs. Patrick was sure he'd died and gone to heaven when she caressed the length of him and ran her thumb over the head of his penis, spreading the pre-cum over his hot flesh. He closed his eyes and gasped as she began a rhythmic stroking.

How long had it been since he'd felt a woman's touch? When was the last time he'd been pleasured with a hand that wasn't his own? He couldn't recall, and tears burned the backs of his lids. Refusing to wallow in the lonely memories, he opened his eyes and met her desirous gaze.

"If you only knew how feckin' good that felt, you'd probably stop to save me the shame of coming early."

She grinned. "Is it shameful to get off when it feels so good? It'll let you last longer when it's your turn to give me pleasure."

"Feck if you aren't the most understanding and wisest woman I've met."

With a laugh, she kissed him. And Patrick experienced a familiarity with her that he'd never had with another. A coming home of sorts. He lost himself completely in the moment.

"Hello?"

They both froze at the call echoing down the corridor.

"Hello? Is there somebody there?"

Fionola retracted her hand so fast his cock flopped out of his pants, causing him to wince when the sensitive skin scraped the zipper's teeth.

"Have a care, love," he warned.

"Oh! Beg your pardon, I—"

"Hello?"

She frowned and tilted her head before rushing toward the sound.

"*Tadhg?* Tadhg, is that you?"

When she pressed against the wall closest to the bars, Patrick's heart tripped.

"Careful!" he shouted, hurrying to put himself to rights and prevent her from touching the bars.

WITH A DISMISSIVE WAVE of her hand, Fi contorted to see down the hallway.

"Fi? Fi! Are ya here to rescue me, then?"

Her heart thudded in her chest, and relief swamped her.

Her brother was alive!

"Tadhg, which end of the hall are you? Your voice is echoing, and I can't tell."

"I'm farthest from the exit," he hollered back. "Did you only just get here, sister? Are ya alone?"

"No, I'm here with Patrick O'Malley. He—"

She heard her brother's vicious swear right before a high-pitched ringing consumed her mind. The sound reverberated, drowning out anything else Tadhg might've said. Clamping her hands over her ears, she cried out.

Patrick's arms encircled her, and he drew her back against his chest. The instant they touched, the noise dissolved into a faint buzz.

"Fi! Can ya hear me, love? Are you all right?" he demanded.

She shoved away from him without responding to his question. The important thing was her brother.

"Tadhg?"

The silence caused her heart to seize.

"Tadhg? Answer me!"

Nothing.

Fi turned stricken eyes to Patrick. "What happened? Why isn't he answering?"

"Who?"

"Tadhg. You had to hear him, yeah?"

When Patrick hesitated, then slowly shook his head, Fi's jaw dropped. Shock caused her face to go numb.

"How is that possible?" She hadn't realized she'd said it aloud until he touched her cheek.

"What is it, love? What did you hear?"

"My brother. He was calling to me, Patrick. He's here, just down the hall!" Frantic, she searched his expression for some sign she wasn't losing her mind. "Are you telling me you heard nothing?"

"I'm sorry, love."

She fell to the floor, stunned and unable to process what had just happened. "He was there! I heard him."

"No." Any telling emotion was smoothed from his face, but a wild, panicked look entered his eyes, and the irises were darker than mere moments before. "I only heard you calling for your brother."

She recognized the reaction. One didn't get to her age without encountering falsehoods and the tools who tossed them out like candy at a parade.

"You're lying," she accused. Building steam, she surged to her feet and gripped the front of his shirt, scattering buttons in every direction when he stepped backward as if to avoid her wrath. "You heard him."

His mouth set in a stubborn line. "I didn't."

"You know more than you're saying, Patrick O'Malley, and if you want to live to see another sunrise, you'd best be telling me what it is you know."

His humor flared, but he immediately tempered it in the face of her building rage. She supposed a man who'd been married understood the way of it when a woman was about to hand him his arse.

"I heard *someone* call out," he finally admitted. "But no more after you said your brother's name. I'd a ringing in my ears, and when it stopped, you were holding your head."

"But you *did* hear him call out first, yeah?"

"I heard something, aye."

Simmering inside, Fi walked to the cell opening. The desire to rattle the metal bars was overwhelming, but the resulting injury would be too severe and not worth the agony inflicted upon herself. Especially when she'd rather inflict harm on Patrick O'Malley!

Why had he lied? It didn't sit well with her after he'd promised he wouldn't. But he'd hidden the truth for a reason, and she intended to find out what it was.

"Fi?" Patrick walked up behind her.

"Yeah?"

"Can I give you my truth?"

The deep timbre of his voice, combined with his tentativeness, caressed her ears and washed away her fury. With a tired sigh, she faced him. "Speak."

His lips twitched, as if her response amused him, but he wore his sincerity like a cloak.

"When we kissed, I was lost in the moment. Many a time I've questioned if an experience is real." Lifting his shaking hands, he examined them before running trembling fingers through his hair. "Likely it comes from being caged alone as long as I've been, but my mind likes to play tricks on me."

"But you promised you'd not lie, and you did."

"Aye, I lied."

His remorse caused her to ask, "Why not just tell me what you heard and trust in me not to think less of you if it wasn't real?"

"Because sometimes I think I'm still Loman's prisoner, and

you're a figment of my imagination, too," he said hoarsely. "That I'm standing here, conversing with an empty room, trying to hang on to the last of my sanity."

"Oh, Patrick." Tenderness swamped her, and she reached for him. When he hesitated to return her hug, Fi squeezed her eyes shut and held on, taking comfort when he relaxed into her embrace and offering whatever solace she could.

"I'm sorry I held back, love. I had to work through what my senses were telling me before I acknowledged that reality."

She drew back and cupped his face, applying a light pressure with her nails.

"Feel that?" When he nodded, she did, too. "It's real. *I'm* real. If you ever question it, I'll help ground you."

Tears shimmered in his incredible eyes, making the jeweled tone brighter before he rapidly blinked them away. He covered her hands, shifting one to his lips and kissing her knuckles.

Fi understood what it was to be overcome with emotion, to be unable to speak for fear of regurgitating all her feelings all over the person with her. There had been many instances where she'd barely contained herself. Patrick didn't need to tell her what was in his heart when she could clearly see it for herself.

"We should probably clean this mess up." She knelt next to the food and began piling the dishes, hoping to allow him time to gather himself. It's what she'd need if the situation were reversed.

Squatting next to her, Patrick stilled her hands. "I've got this."

With a wave, it was gone. Their meal, the plates, the silverware, and the napkins. All of it! Even the buttons she'd scattered about the room were back on his shirt as if they'd never been ripped off.

Fi froze in place with her heart thundering in her chest.

He'd used magic without it backfiring! Effortlessly!

CHAPTER 13

This chapter has been omitted as per T.M.'s time-honored tradition. You're encouraged to jump up, stretch a little, and perhaps grab snacks for the next half of this story. Also, now's a great time to consider whether or not you'd like another installment of The Unlucky Charms after this one. Be sure to continue reading when the story is concluded to find the link and vote yay or nay.

CHAPTER 14

*P*atrick had screwed up. Somehow, in some small way, he'd triggered Fionola, but he'd be buggered if he could recall exactly what he'd said or done. Whenever he approached her, she would tense up and move away. At times, subtly. At others, not so much. Seeing her closed off to him created a tightness in his chest that refused to ease.

To afford her as much space as possible, he'd let her have the bed and had settled in his usual spot in the far back corner of the room, away from the light. The coward in him didn't dare ask, but the tension was growing thicker by the minute, and he felt a driving need to clear the air.

If only to breathe freely again.

"What is it you think I've done, love?" he asked from his comfort zone.

Whenever Loman walked the aisles and taunted his victims, Patrick had shifted into the shadows to hide his instinctive reaction. The hatred he'd felt for the man was always plain for all to see, and it gave that gobshite too much pleasure to witness it. To deny his enemy the satisfaction, Patrick learned to lurk in the darkness.

Old habits died hard.

"Nothing." Fi's chin was raised in defiance, but her eyes were wary, as if she suspected him of nefarious activity. She'd monitored his every movement from the moment their kiss was interrupted.

"Sure, and normally I'd let that stick, but we all know when a woman says 'nothing' in that tone, it's something," he teased.

Her head whipped in his direction, and a storm cloud settled on her features.

Ah, fuck! Sure, and he'd stepped in shite now!

Patrick sighed, prepared to take whatever lumps she intended to dole out. That's what he got for being a eejit in the face of her anger.

"Your magic worked!" she shouted, sounding accusing.

"Wha—" His jaw dropped as the realization she was right sunk in.

Gobsmacked, he surveyed the room. Not a single spec of food or dirt to be found!

Meeting her salty stare, he shook his head. "I didn't know, Fi. It never occurred to me that it had. I'm sorry."

"How is it possible after all the exploding food?"

Sharp pain started behind his eyes, and he closed his lids to fight off the sudden throbbing ache. The ringing began in his ears again, and he covered them to drown out the sound. Pressure built, and it felt as if his brain were about to explode. He cried out in his agony.

"Patrick?" Fi's voice came from beside him. When he dared open his eyes, she was there, looking worried but also as if she suspected him of acting.

His heart thudded in time to the pulsing pain in his skull.

"I'm grand," he said.

"You sure?"

"Aye," he lied.

"Right. So if your powers are in full force, you should try to get us out of here, then." Her tone was grudging, as if she still didn't trust him, but was willing to pretend if it achieved her goal of freedom.

His chest tightened further. Why did women always want to escape his presence? Was he so undesirable? Was he so unskilled in his advances that he turned others off? It bore further thinking about, but he'd be damned if he'd ask Fi, not when she looked at him as if he were about to abscond with her family's silver.

Clearing his throat, he stood and, concentrating on placing one foot in front of the other, crossed to the center of their cell. "Aye. Come, and I'll try to send you home, yeah?"

She scrambled to her feet—too fast for his liking—but Patrick remained mute on the subject. Once she placed her palms in his, he shut his eyes, closing out the distrust she exhibited.

"Dear Anu, hear my plea,
assist me in this time of need.
Release Fionola from this place,
and take her where she'll be safe."

Light filled the room, and a crack appeared in the fabric of space. Through the slit, Fionola's small village appeared to grow closer. If one squinted, they could see Noah Fucking Riley's place in the distance.

The thought of her returning to the pub owner soured his stomach.

"Wait!" she cried.

Patrick was unprepared for the impact of her body with his, and he stumbled backward with his arms full of Fi. Maintaining the spell was impossible, and the portal sealed shut with a snap and a fizzle.

"For fuck's sake, woman! Do you not have the sense the

Goddess gave a feckin' mule?" He set her aside and began to pace. His blood pressure shot up, doing nothing to ease the ache in his head. "You'd have had your wish to be away from me, and what do ya do? You feckin' ruined it, ya did! *Are ya mad?*"

After blocking his path, she gave a vicious shove to his chest and settled her fists on her hips. She was stunning in her fury. "Don't speak to me like that, ya lug!"

An incredulous snort escaped him, but he kept his mouth shut because what he wanted to say would blister her ears. Even a low-level witch knew better than to interrupt a casting the way Fionola had.

"You did it wrong," she said in a haughty voice.

Frustrated beyond measure—and not just about a spell gone wrong—Patrick's jaw clamped. Not only did he fear for the welfare of his molars, but he was certain his head was about to explode. Still, there were worse things than dying of one quick brain splat.

"Did ya hear me?" she demanded.

"Aye," he snapped. If he didn't wring her neck before the day was through, he'd be grand. When he could speak again without spitting teeth, he asked, "And what, pray tell, did I do wrong, O' Wise One?"

Her lips compressed in a tight line, and her eyes were troubled.

His anger dissolved in the face of her upset.

"Fi? What did I do wrong?" For the life of him, he didn't understand. If he'd missed something and created a portal to harm her, he'd never forgive himself.

"You weren't going to save yourself," she whispered. "Just me."

As confused as when their argument had started, he pressed his temples, wishing he could go back into the shadows and ease his aching head. How hard was it to please one woman? Why couldn't he do anything right?

"And that's why you stopped me?" he asked. "Because you didn't want to go through the portal alone?"

"No, I…" The look she cast the cell door was helpless. "I'm sorry. I can't go without my brother."

Patrick's stomach bottomed out. How had he forgotten? Jaysus, he was a bloody old fool.

"Your brother," he stated flatly. "Aye."

"He's who we came to find," she reminded him, though he wasn't likely to forget again. Fi was here for Tadhg, not him.

"I'm after trying the spell again, yeah, and I don't expect you to stop it this time. If the opportunity arises, you're to escape, Fionola Bohannon, and not spare another thought for those left behind." When her lips formed a protest, he covered them with his index finger. "I'll save your brother, love. I promise I'll find a way to tear down this place and get him out."

"Thank you!" She rushed into his arms, hugging him tightly around the waist. And really, he had no choice but to embrace her. His heart wouldn't let him push her away, though it would be for the best if he did.

"I'm sorry, Patrick."

"You've no need to be, but have a care around active magic in the future, yeah?" he said gruffly.

Lifting her face up, she grinned. "You always turn grumbly whenever your softer side makes an appearance."

"It's because my softer side dumps me in the deepest water without a life preserver. It's a fucking pain in my arse." Digging deep into his reserves, he found the strength to set her from him. Sure, his brain understood she was only here for Tadhg, but his body and heart hadn't received the message, and they were both begging him to claim her for his own.

———

Noah scried for the fifth time in two hours to no avail. Neither Fi nor Patrick appeared anywhere on the map. Frustrated, he blew out a breath. Needing a break from the family drama, he'd left his brother and niece behind with the O'Malleys to work on the problem. Noah was better with solo endeavors, and he was determined to find Fi as soon as humanly possible.

A knock sounded on his pub door, and he frowned at the intrusion. With a wave of his hand, he unlocked and opened it, not bothering to cross the room. Indeed, he'd recognized his visitor the instant his face appeared on the other side of the aged and distorted glass.

"What do you want, Aether?"

Damian clasped his hands behind his back and ignored Noah to meander around the room. Here and there, he paused to study a picture on the wall or run his fingertips across a beautifully crafted furniture piece. He strolled the place as if he didn't have a care in the world and nowhere to be.

"I asked what ya wanted," Noah ground out.

"To see where you live. Your place of business," Damian replied smoothly, with no outward sign of irritation.

He, on the other hand, was annoyed enough for the both of them. "You're not welcome here."

That stopped the Aether in his tracks. Pivoting, he met Noah's challenging stare, and the fucker had the nerve to smile. The action wasn't taunting or mean, but held the warmth of the sun.

"Growing up, I'd always wanted a bratty little brother. One who I could say wasn't an adopted sibling," Damian told him. "You'd have fit the bill nicely, I believe."

With a snort, he crossed his arms. "Well, I suppose it's too feckin' bad our mother went mad and you're filled with evil, yeah?"

His retort wiped all expression from his brother's smug face.

"What is it you believe you know about me, Noah? I've the distinct impression our father didn't provide you with the pertinent details."

"Damarius was a lot of things, most of them mean, but he wasn't a liar."

"Mean?" A frown furrowed Damian's brow. "Father was only disagreeable during the time he was infected by the Darkness, but Mother removed it."

"Disagreeable. Ha! That's rich. It had little to do with any residual Darkness, to be sure." To put distance between them, he walked behind the bar and picked up a pint glass. After lifting it as an offering and receiving Damian's nod, he drew a Guinness for each of them. "His soul took the beating, and he never recovered from the loss of you and our mother. When the man wasn't crying in his cups, he was berating me for not being *you*."

"I'm sorry."

Noah's brows shot up, but the sympathy on Damian's face made him uncomfortable, and he shrugged. "What are you apologizing for? He's the one who fled his home. I'd probably have suffered less if he'd left me behind for her to murder me."

The temperature in the room cooled, and when he glanced up, it was to see his brother's arch look.

"She wouldn't have," Damian said sharply. "She didn't murder me, and she wouldn't have harmed her baby."

"That's not the word on the street." Yes, he was pushing buttons, but Noah needed to gauge the man beneath the power. To really see what he was made of, and not be subjected to the act he presented to the world.

"I don't care what the word is. She wouldn't have hurt you. With the last of her willpower, she requested assistance on my behalf." Damian picked up his drink and studied the contents.

"If you were with us, she'd have sent you away with me. But the fact she let Father take you once she'd become infected spoke of her love for you."

In two centuries of living, Noah had never considered it from Damian's point of view. And although his mother might've actually cared about him, he found it hard to reconcile the past with the present.

"Perhaps," he finally said, removing Damian's drink from his hand to take a sip and hand it back. "If I wanted to poison you, I'd have done it already."

His brother laughed and placed the drink on the bar top. "I'm not much of a beer drinker. I prefer an aged scotch or brandy."

"Well why the feck didn't ya say so?" Noah shot him a disgusted look and reached for a bottle on the top shelf. "Feckin' pretty manners," he scoffed. "You need to live in the wilds of Ireland for a time, then ya'd speak plain."

"I lived in the wilds of America during my youth. Trust me. I have the ability to get down and dirty with the best of them. But I prefer civilized conversations and finer things as I get older."

"Aye, and you're ancient." After serving up a tumbler of his best scotch, Noah downed the remainder of the beer, then swiped his shirtsleeve across his mouth to wipe away the foam before offering up a hearty belch.

Damian merely laughed at his antics. "Like I said, I'd have appreciated a bratty younger brother." The Aether's mood shifted. "My daughter revealed some truths after you left, Noah. If you care to hear them, I'll tell you what I know."

"What happened to the rules you hammered the wild beastie with? Is it fair they don't apply to you, then?"

Obsidian eyes, so solemn yet sincere, stared back at him, waiting.

"Fuck it." Noah drank the second pint and set the glass on the bar. "Fine. Out with it."

"She said Fionola won't return to you."

He scowled at Damian. "And what the bleedin' hell does that mean? To work, to this village, to me in particular?"

"I took it to mean *you*, but Beastie can be quite literal. It may mean to the village or even to work here, I suppose."

"And did your child-clone tell you we'd find her?"

"Yes, but not right away or without a great deal of effort."

"Jaysus. If I'd known I was supposed to be solving riddles, I'd have kept a clear head," Noah muttered.

Damian's mouth quirked up on one side. "I've more bad news for you."

"Of course you do."

"My wife would like to have you over for dinner tonight. I'm not to return home without your agreement."

With a scowl, Noah gathered the glasses and began to wash up. "Why me? And why tonight?"

"You, because you're family. Tonight, because Vivian can be as impatient as our children."

Curious despite himself, he studied Damian. "Your daughter mentioned she had a brother."

"Nate. Named after my foster father, Nathanial Thorne." There was sadness in the his brother's smile. "He was a great man, and I wish you could've had him for a father."

Noah was astonished to realize Damian was sad because Nathanial hadn't raised him, too. He did the only thing he could to cover his surprise—he agreed to dinner.

CHAPTER 15

After his brother left, Noah returned to the table holding his scrying supplies. Cursing himself for forgetting to ask Damian to give it a try, he picked up the crystal. Whatever it took, he'd find her. And he'd give no credence to Sabrina's prediction that he and Fi wouldn't be together. He loved her, and she loved him. They were meant to be, and he'd be quick to provide anyone who disagreed what for!

Outside the door, a commotion arose, and he ran to check it out. Townspeople milled in the street and were pointing at a golden streak suspended on the hill, as if lightning was frozen in the middle of a strike. Those unfamiliar with teleportation would assume a natural phenomenon. But those in the witch community knew better, and he met the gaze of a tiny, hunchbacked elderly woman with rheumy purple eyes, the same color as her disturbing lavender hair. The soft glow of her aura indicated she was a witch, and she watched him with the same curiosity as he did her. Oversized dentures shifted around her mouth when she suddenly grinned at him. With a stubby, gnarled finger, she shoved them back in place, chomping down twice then following it up with pat of her coiffed hair and a hand dusting.

"What do you make of that, boy?" she asked in an American accent. It held the slightest twang, as if she were somewhere from the southern half of the country.

Part of him questioned whether she was referring to the light on the hill or her wayward false teeth.

"Do you know me, then?" he asked in reply. It paid to be careful. His mother had acquired many enemies in her lifetime.

Her grin widened, and her top denture flopped to the bottom of her mouth. Noah winced on her behalf. Getting old sucked, even for witches—*wait a fecking minute!* Witches didn't age to such a degree unless they were hundreds of years old. And as far as he knew, his brother and him were the oldest.

Eyes narrowed, he approached her. "Who are ya, and why the disguise?"

"I've no idea what you're talking about. I'm just a tourist visiting a quaint little town."

The sparkle in her purple peepers said differently.

"Are you here to spy on me? Or are you after something else?" he demanded in a steely tone, but he didn't feel anything remotely close to evil intent radiating from her. Merely mischief.

"Young'uns today are a suspicious lot." She sighed. "Looks like the light show is over. Pour me a drink so I can get off these old feet of mine, why don't you?"

Keeping his senses sharp against an attack, he led the way into his pub, shutting the door after she entered and drawing down the shade. Facing her, he crossed his arms and narrowed his eyes to show he meant business.

"Lose the disguise."

The blinding light caused by her change nearly seared his eyelids shut and forced him to throw his arms up as a shield. The blonde bombshell who stood in the old woman's place unhinged his jaw. She resembled an eighties movie star with her thick wavy hair, skintight lavender top, white palazzo pants, and chunky gold jewelry. A look she pulled off effortlessly.

"Much more comfortable," she said as she sauntered to the bar.

"Who are you?"

"My name's GiGi Gillespie."

"Doesn't mean anything to me," he told her.

"No? Perhaps I should tack on my maiden name. *Thorne.*"

Having heard the Thorne name less than an hour before from his brother, Noah frowned. There was no such thing as coincidence in the magical world. "And how are you related to Nathanial?"

"You knew Nathanial?" When he shook his head, she shrugged as if she didn't care one way or the other. "He was my great-grandfather. But you might be more familiar with my brother. Alastair Thorne."

Everyone who possessed an iota of magic knew of Alastair, and not a single one of those people wanted to be on the man's radar. If his sister was here, that meant Noah was now a blip on Alastair's. He mentally cursed at failing to make the connection between Nathanial and her brother.

"Sure, and I've heard of him. Who hasn't?" Casually, he meandered around the bar and removed a clean wineglass from the shelf. "Your drink is Merlot, aye?"

He prided himself on knowing these things. Earlier, he'd poured the Guinness for Damian simply to annoy him and force him to drink what he didn't like.

"Yes. A Merlot would be lovely. Thank you." She turned and sashayed to the table with the scrying map and crystals, her curvy hips swishing from side to side in a way that drew a man's eye without fail. Just like they drew Noah's. She turned as he approached, accepting the glass with a sunny smile.

"To what do I owe the honor of your visit, GiGi Thorne-Gillespie? I'm assuming you're here for a reason, yeah?"

She gave another delicate shrug of her shoulder. "Bridget O'Malley is part of my coven. She's worried about you but didn't have the resources to spare to check on you. Apparently, she's trying to locate her father."

"Aye, as I'm trying to locate my girlfriend, who's with him."

GiGi's mouth twisted in a smirk. "Well, I'm surprised your girlfriend left you for Patrick, though he *is* a good-looking fella. But maybe she prefers someone a little less... *broody*."

"She didn't leave me for *him*," Noah snapped. "And that man is a whole helluva lot broodier than me, he is! She left me to find her brother—"

Her brother!

Of course!

If Noah couldn't find Fi, he could scry for Tadhg. Wherever he was, Fi was sure to end up. A more relentless person than Fionola Bohannon never existed.

"You can tell Bridget I'm grand. But I've work to do, so if you don't mind, take the wine and go."

"Wow. You'd think someone who owns a public establishment would be a little friendlier to their patrons." Without seeming to care he was in a rush, she sipped her drink and set it on the table. Then she leaned over and began examining the map. "Would you like my help? My magic will amplify yours if we work together."

As a loner with only a basic skillset, Noah had never participated in ceremonies other than for the initial learning. He'd seen how some people combined their abilities to achieve a goal, but he'd never dared be that close to someone. Merging magic spoke of familiarity he didn't care for, and there was no telling what might happen if someone encountered his bound power.

But it was Fi. And he'd just sworn to himself he'd do whatever it took to find her.

"Were you the one who caused the light on the hill?" he asked, stalling for time and because he wanted to know.

GiGi dropped her friendly act, and her gaze was frank when it met his. "No. If I had to guess, it was an aborted teleport. Whose, I don't know, but it can't be good if someone was performing magic and got cut off."

"Aye. I'd a similar thought." He rubbed the back of his neck as he considered the problem. "It might've been Fi."

"If it was, you need to find her right away."

"Do you think I haven't been trying?" He waved a hand toward the table's surface, encompassing the entire contents. "Does it look like I've been sitting on me arse?"

GiGi laughed, and the musical sound grated on his last nerve.

"Come, Noah. I've a surefire way of finding your friend." She finished the last of her wine and set it on the bar top. "But it's not here."

"I've somewhere to be in one hour." As soon as he said it, he regretted it, because he'd ignore the Aether's invitation in a second if it meant finding Fi.

"Oh, and where's that?"

"The Dethr—" He stopped, silently cursing himself for almost giving away his connection to Damian. They bore too strong a resemblance for someone not to take note if he bandied the name around. Clearly he couldn't say "brother's house" either because he wasn't feeling particularly familial in relation to his newfound family.

She studied him through narrowed eyes and nodded. "If I had to guess, I'd say, based on your coloring, that you're related to Damian Dethridge or Sebastian Drake. And since I'm positive you intended to say Dethridge, I'd also venture you don't want anyone to know about it."

Noah's brows slammed together, and he refused to answer. How the hell had she guessed what he intended to say? Fuck all if he wasn't losing his touch.

Her smile was triumphant. "It speaks well of you to not put your family in danger, but Damian and the Thornes go way back. Where we're going isn't too far from Ravenswood."

Ravenswood.

The family seat of the Dethridge family. *His* family if he chose to claim them. They certainly seemed willing to embrace him.

When Noah remained undecided, GiGi slipped a phone from the pocket of her flowy white pants.

"Damian, GiGi here." She listened for a moment, then laughed. "Actually, I'm with your brother, Noah."

"I didn't tell ya we were brothers." Taking a step back, Noah scowled at her. "Where—"

She rolled her eyes and waved him off as if he were a pesky child. "Bridget," she mouthed as she listened to whatever Damian was saying. "Yes, of course. I was about to take him to the Death Garden by the Drake estate. I thought the standing stones might give us the magical boost needed to find his lady love," she said into the phone, offering Noah a wink in the process. "Right. We'll meet you there in a few minutes. Ta!"

After disconnecting and slipping the phone back into her pocket, she held out her hand and wiggled her fingers. "Come, darling boy. We've got an appointment with the Aether."

"I'm older than you," Noah said dryly, placing his palm in hers.

"Really? Hmm. You're remarkably well preserved."

There was no time to retort, and the next thing he knew, he was standing in front of a tombstone etched with his mother's name. His shock was great.

CHAPTER 16

Tadhg slammed his hands against the bars of his cell, frustrated he'd missed the opportunity to tell Fionola what had happened to him. Knowing her as he did, he had no doubt she'd called Patrick O'Malley to help find him and wound up in a world of trouble because of it.

"This fucking place!"

A breeze swept the room, and Tadhg drew back into the shadows. The habit of hiding from Loman O'Connor had never left him, but it had come in handy until he was caught this week. All those months, he'd begun to believe he was paranoid, as his family seemed to suspect. Yet he'd been right. Someone was stalking and abducting all the unwilling victims of this godforsaken prison and returning them to their original jail cells.

And he knew exactly who that someone was.

"You're not to speak to the woman again, or it'll go worse for ya," the hooded figure growled.

"Fuck off, why don't ya!" Tadhg snapped.

The material dropped down, exposing the man's head and

strong facial features. His eyes were glowing with fury. "I'll not say it again."

A shiver chased along Tadhg's spine, but he held his chin high as he moved forward. He wrapped a hand around one of the metal bars and shook it.

"Why not supercharge it like Loman? Steal our magic to fuel yours?"

"I'm no thief."

"No. Just a fucking liar and kidnapper, aye?"

The man's scowl held confusion, and he shook his head slowly. "There's an order to things. A rightful place. This is where we belong."

He caught the man's slip. *"We?"*

"Just keep your gob shut. No more noise out of you, boy."

"I'm no boy, and when I get out of here—"

"You're not getting out unless I let you out."

"I swear—" Tadhg's next words were cut off with a strangled cry, and as he struggled to draw a breath, his captor shook his fist. The invisible hand on his neck squeezed and caused Tadhg to reach out beseechingly.

It took strong magic to choke another without laying a finger on them, and the man in front of him held an impressive amount. Tadhg's standard allotment was a pittance in comparison.

As dark spots danced in his periphery, he grew dizzy and fell into the wall, sliding down to land on his hip with a painful thud. The impact would leave a bruise, but it was the least of his worries. His most pressing need was air.

He was seconds from death when the man's fist opened, releasing Tadhg to gulp in oxygen through coughing fits.

"Remember what I told you. Don't talk to the woman."

Speaking was painful, but he refused to be cowered. "If you hurt her—"

"Hush your whist," the man said, albeit a little gentler and with a grim expression. "I'm not after hurting your sister, or anyone, for that matter."

Yeah, and hadn't he just about crushed Tadhg's windpipe? The man was cracked in the head, and Tadhg needed to remember to tread carefully until such a time he could gain the upper hand.

"How much longer are you planning to keep us here?" he asked in a neutral tone.

The man's mouth thinned into a flat, white line. Frustration simmered in his eyes, and his head rocked back and forth in a negative motion as if Tadhg's question was too much for him.

"You're not a bad man," he told his captor, lying through his teeth. Anyone who would abduct and re-imprison another lunatic's previous victims was just as evil in his book. "I know you're not. I've seen—"

"*Stop. Talking!*"

"Don't hurt my sister. *Please.*"

The man pulled up the hood, hiding his close-cropped graying hair, and drew the front low to keep his face in shadow. "Behave, Tadhg Bohannon. If I have to come back, I'll not be happy with ya."

"I'm trembling in me boots," Tadhg sneered. And he really was, but he'd be buggered if he'd admit it.

A grin flashed on the other man's face, and it was almost friendly in nature. "You're a lot like her, to be sure."

PATRICK AWOKE WITH A START, disoriented and bordering on panicked. The instant he sensed Fi, curled against him like the snuggle bug she was, the tension left his body. Only with her did he feel normal. Feel as if he were able to sleep nightmare-free for as long as he liked and without waking as if his body was a thousand years old. With her, the future might not be a scary place to exist, after all. But she wouldn't stay. He knew this with a certainty unmatched by any optimism he could muster.

He scrubbed his free hand over his face and winced when he encountered the stubble. A shave was paramount. If she ever took it into her head to kiss him again, the scratching of her lovely skin would be a goddamned tragedy. Likely she wouldn't, though, and that was a crying shame.

The hope he felt around her was a double-edged sword. His desire for her bordered desperation, but his sense of self-preservation called him a fool at every turn. Instinctively, he understood that if he fell for Fionola fully and she left him after a night of true intimacy, she'd destroy him in a way Rose's defection never could.

Fi murmured something in her sleep and wiggled closer, wedging herself under his arm and resting her silky-soft cheek on his bare chest. She locked him in place with her shapely leg over his. Goddess, what he wouldn't give to have free rein to run his hands along her smooth skin. To touch her hot core, that he felt even now through the material of his pant leg. To taste her everywhere, leaving no spot unexplored.

His hard-on was past the point of painful, and as much as he wanted to adjust his dick to a more comfortable position, he didn't want to be caught seemingly fondling himself if she woke up. Patrick almost laughed at the ridiculousness of his situation. He was mad for a woman who was years younger and in love with another man, but who was also trapped with *him* for the foreseeable future. What he was beginning to feel for her was a thousand times more powerful than what he'd felt for Rose all those years ago. Or maybe it was the same, but his wife's betrayal had tainted his memories.

A sudden clawing need to break free bubbled up inside him. If he didn't, he might do something truly asinine like lay his heart at Fi's feet for her to trample all over as she ran to Noah or Tadhg or any number of people not him.

Patrick released a slow breath.

Aye, he was unlovable. He should've understood the message the first time his wife had told him. With his index finger, he jabbed his forehead three times.

"Remember that, remember that, remember that," he silently chanted. *"Quit being a feckin' eejit, Patrick!"*

Rather than disturb Fi, he teleported from the bed to the corner of the room. Backing into the shadows where their excuse for a bathroom existed, he washed his face and scrubbed his teeth, using the toothbrush and paste their captor had seen fit to leave them.

They'd been left to rot, but their teeth sure as hell wouldn't. When their dried-out husks were found, Patrick imagined their chompers would be blinding white in their ghastly, open-mouthed grins so at odds with their grotesque corpses.

He snorted at his absurd gallows humor. Over the years, he'd become a pro at turning his unlucky circumstances into laughable situations. Although he doubted anyone else would appreciate his dark wit.

In the mirror, he glanced at the bed.

Fionola might.

During their mundane conversations, she'd laughed and returned his snark word for word. Her stories were filled with the same dark humor as his.

Giving into his overwhelming need, Patrick turned and rested his butt against the sink. He crossed his ankles and arms, then proceeded to watch her sleep. What did it say about him that he could make a pastime of observing her? Was he a voyeur at heart, or just a sucker for love?

Her strawberry-blonde hair was a mass of tangles, spread over her shoulders and pouring down her back. She'd shifted after he left and was now on her stomach, curled into a pillow, hugging it as she had him. One leg remained hiked up, as it had been when she'd pinned him to the mattress, and the sheet rode low on her hips. Hips he'd pay to see naked. Hell, unteachable fool that he was, he'd give his very soul for one night with her.

It took him a solid ten seconds to register that she was watching him as he was her, and his heart thudded painfully in his chest the instant he noted the bold light of intent in her eyes. Only, he didn't know what that intent meant. Once, he'd have believed it was desire. But his ability to discern a woman's thoughts had never been on point.

His stomach clenched in anticipation as she shifted into a sitting position and swung the bedsheet back. On bare feet, she padded to him, and her eyes dropped to view his chest, making him acutely aware he'd never put his shirt on after washing up. Then her gaze lowered to the outline of his thickening penis.

Probably he should apologize for his morning wood, but she was old enough to understand a man's reaction wasn't always voluntary when he saw a beautiful woman in dishabille.

"Good morning." Her voice, unused from hours of sleep, was husky and inviting.

"Good mornin', love."

Her mouth kicked up in the corners as if she was pleased by his endearment.

No one was more surprised than him when she reached out and ran a hand down the center of his bare chest, trailing her fingers through the hair leading to the waistband of his pants.

Hooking a finger in the top, she lazily lifted her lids and met his unblinking gaze. His only hope was that he didn't appear as desperate as he felt. Inside, he was a bundle of raw nerves, wondering if he still had it in him to please a woman like her. He also knew that despite the fact he'd be broken and battered when she sauntered her lovely arse back to Noah, he'd take whatever she offered and be appreciative of it.

"You've had this for quite some time, Patrick O'Malley. Should we take care of it?"

"That depends what you mean, love. If it's chopping the bleedin' thing off, I'll have to deny ya."

She laughed as she shifted closer and nuzzled his nipple. After swiping her tongue across it, she closed her mouth over the tight bud and suckled. Pleasure shot straight to his groin, and his cock turned as hard as Connemara marble. As if she knew exactly what result she'd caused, Fi ran her hand under his waistband and along the length of him.

"I'm not after chopping anything off, Patrick. I admire the feel of it too much."

He groaned. "Are ya sure you're wanting to start something here, love? It's not as if we have privacy."

She lifted her head, bringing a halt to the exploration of her mouth on his chest. With a frown, she glanced toward the cell door. "If we can't hear anyone else, can they possibly hear us?"

"I've never known this place to be soundproof before you got here, so I can't answer you with any honesty."

"You've magic. Can you cloak us for a short while?"

Patrick visually followed the motion of his fingers as he brushed a lock of hair from her flushed face. "Do you believe this is a grand plan, Fionola? Mind you, it's not no I'm saying, but would you feel as amorous on the outside?"

Her fingers tightened around him, and his eyes nearly rolled back in his head his pleasure was so great.

"I believe it's a grand ride we'll be having. But if you're not interested…" As she began to withdraw, he clasped her wrist, holding her in place.

"Now don't be hasty, woman! If you say it's a grand ride, then I'm as interested as can be."

She laughingly led him to the bed.

CHAPTER 17

Fi braced her forearms on Patrick's chest and grinned down at him. His face was more relaxed than she'd ever seen, and the soft glow in his eyes was solely for her. The rhythmic stroking of his fingers along her spine caused her blood to thrum through her veins and amorous feelings to build again. After the ride they'd shared, she wasn't certain once would be enough.

"I'm beginning to like it here," she confessed. "With the exception of my worry for Tadhg, I could spend every day trading stories, stealing the tastiest bits of food, and licking Belgian chocolate off your skin."

She felt his chuckle in her sternum, and when he lovingly brushed back her sweat-dampened hair, all her insides turned to goo. It had become a habitual gesture of his, and she was growing fond of the feeling his absent-minded action created.

"And I'd treasure each of those days if we had them," he assured her.

Noah, practical and work-minded as he was, would never say something so sweet in return. He'd have laughed off her fantasy, smacked her bare arse, and told her he had to place an order for the pub.

But Patrick was proving to be a dreamer, like her. Sure, it wasn't practical for two dreamers to coexist, but it did lend to romance in place of practicality. And Fi desperately longed for some in her mundane life.

"You've a beautiful soul, Patrick O'Malley," she whispered past her thickening throat.

His blissful expression morphed into a troubled one. "Your heart is too soft, love. I'm not worthy of your praise, but damned if I'm not honored by it, all the same."

"Why do you think you don't deserve it? You've been kind to my parents, determined to help me find Tadhg, and even when you're cross, you are gentle and considerate." She traced his frowning brow with her finger, attempting to smooth it. "Yeah, you're a bear when riled, but it doesn't last."

"It doesn't last with *you*," he corrected. "Ask anyone else, and they'll tell you I'm a right proper bastard."

"I don't believe it. Your family holds you in high regard. Their respect for you is endless."

He smiled, soft and sweet. "My children are my blessing. And maybe my curse." He laughed at her gasp. "Cian, he's always looking for mischief, or he was as a child. Carrick is my quiet one. Fell in love with his forever mate when he was but a young boy." Patrick resumed stroking Fi's back. "Bridget, now, she's as fierce as they come. She's been in love with the neighbor boy, Ruairí, for as long as I can remember. In as much as I hate he's an O'Connor, he's probably the one good thing to come from that horrid family."

"And your twins?"

"I didn't get to know them well. I went out for a pack of fags, and on my return home, I was captured by Loman O'Connor. He kept me caged for years, and when I escaped, my family wasn't my own."

"What does that mean? They had to be worried about you?"

"They seemed to be thriving under Bridget's care, and I wasn't in my right mind, able to raise the twins."

"Where did you go?"

"I lived the life of a traveler for a bit. Trying to learn tricks for when I sought revenge on Loman."

"What happened to ya?"

"I lost myself for a time, and I could never get the better of that gobshite. It became my obsession." Patrick sighed, shifted her, and rolled to a sitting position. His legs were bent, tenting the sheet but leaving his slim hip bare, and he leaned forward, draping his arms over his knees. With seemingly unseeing eyes, he stared at his palms as if they'd somehow failed him. "I wanted so badly to kill him, Fi. So fucking badly. But he won, time and again."

He met her gaze, and his was so damned tortured that her heart spasmed.

"How does a mere mortal win against someone who possesses unimaginable power? Against a fucking evil so great they can't comprehend the depths of depravity their enemy will sink to?"

"He sounds horrible."

"Aye. He was. And my youngest has tied her future to the man's son." Patrick balled his fists. "Sure, and you say I've a beautiful soul, but I'd rip him from her life if I could. He'll destroy her one day. Like his father did Rose."

"Rose?"

"Loman sought to tempt her away, and he succeeded." He scoffed and shook his head. "One more strike against the hated O'Malleys."

"But surely she had to know he was using her? How does a woman fall for her husband's sworn enemy?"

"The sworn enemy pretends to be someone he's not to gain her trust." Patrick scrubbed a hand over the back of his head as if to rub away his frustration. "Ronan did the same to Dubheasa. The man has a greater power than his father, and he lives amongst us. If he stays true to the O'Connor form, he'll take down the entire O'Malley clan."

Faced with such a dilemma as his, Fi could well understand why Patrick was distrustful.

"Tadhg told me Ronan was the one to stop his da. That he, along with a Traveler and two Death Dealers, finally ended his reign of terror for good." Fi rubbed Patrick's back, hoping to reassure him. "Maybe he's the opposite of Loman. He's got to be good if your daughter sees something in him, yeah?"

"I don't know."

"The O'Malley family members I've met don't suffer fools. I think they have *you* to thank for that, Paddy O."

He snorted at her new nickname for him.

"I'm trying endearments on for size," she said with a grin.

His impossibly green eyes burned bright as he locked gazes with her. "Endearments are for lovers who have strong emotions for one another. Are you telling me you've developed feelings for me, Fionola Bohannon?"

Never breaking eye contact, she rose to her knees and clasped his face between her hands. "And what if I am?"

"I'd say you could do far better than the likes of me, love."

"And what is 'love' if not an endearment?"

His lips twitched an instant before his knee-weakening grin broke free. "Oh, aye, it's an endearment, to be sure."

"What if I said you could do far better than the likes of me?" she returned.

"I'd tell ya true it will never happen. Not in this lifetime or the next." He reached for her, tumbling her back onto the bed and triggering her happy laughter. For one heart-stopping, poignant moment, he stared down at her, and Fi was able to see his naked longing. It called to her soul, leaving it raw and aching to bond with his. To become true soulmates. She was beginning to suspect Patrick O'Malley was her twin flame.

"This is real," she assured him, remembering his comment about never being certain if his situation was made up or if it was reality.

"I'd like to think so, or I'm going to wake up and find a helluva sticky mess coating the sheets."

CHAPTER 18

"**S**he's not dead."

Noah jerked at the sound of Damian's voice from behind him. He'd been so lost in the wonder of seeing the Enchantress's final resting place that he didn't hear anyone approach.

Isolde de Thorne.

Also known as Isolde Dethridge and defeated only a few years after Noah's birth by a goddess, gods, and what constituted as the Six—the original magical families from both sides of the veil.

"So she's sleeping in there, then? All these centuries later?" The idea of being entombed was enough to give a man claustrophobia. Part of him wanted to rip the cracked marble lid off with his bare hands.

That's when what he was seeing actually sank in.

The lid!

It was damaged.

Horrified, he spun to look at Damian, all the while pointing at the tomb. "It's broken. How has she not escaped?"

"She did. About four years ago. But she parted ways with

the Darkness, which was banished to the Netherworld to wither and die."

"Where is…" The question hung in the back of his throat, choking him. He didn't expect the emotional onslaught for the motherless boy he'd been. For feck's sake, he was older than dirt! Those worthless memories and feelings should mean nothing to him after this length of time.

"It's a long story. One I'm willing to tell you, but bottom line, she's in the Netherworld, too."

"*You* put her there?"

"I needed her help to open the portal between worlds. Mother was my balance, but she chose to remain when our adventure went sideways."

There was tightness in the fine lines around Damian's eyes, but one had to look closely to see it. He hadn't been chuffed to leave her behind, that much was clear.

"Tell me why we're here. For your friend to lull me into a trap?" Noah was no match for the Aether or the witch when it came to magic, but he could land a vicious punch when needed.

His brother released a tired sigh as he approached. "Your distrust is exhausting, brother. Dial it down a bit and read the room, won't you?"

With a suspicious glance at the vivacious woman, who was unnaturally silent, Noah backed up a few steps to create distance. No one spoke as he inhaled and exhaled the four long, cleansing breaths to center himself. When he was calmer, he drew his minuscule magic from deep within his cells, pushed it to the surface, and sent out feelers to gauge the others' emotions and intent.

He found nothing but concern.

For him!

Other than Fi, no one had given a shite about him in too many years to count, and he didn't know how to process the information.

"No one here is your enemy, Noah," Damian said. Honesty radiated off him, impossible to deny.

"I don't have power for you to steal," he warned.

A smile teased his brother's mouth, making it appear as if he held back laughter. "I'm well aware."

"Aye. I suppose you are." Feeling like an eejit, Noah hunched his shoulders and shoved his hands deep into his jeans pockets, belatedly realizing he hadn't changed into formal attire for the Dethridges' dinner party. "So, why am I here?"

"This private garden used to contain our mother. Far beneath the surface are the standing stones that kept her in stasis. They're capable of doing much more." As Damian spoke, he circled the perimeter until he was in front of him. "One minor spell from me, and they'll rise from the ground and activate."

"I still don't understand what any of this has to do with me."

"Two things, really. First, it will amplify the power GiGi provides you and help you find your lady friend." He held up a hand. "Before you ask why I can't assist you personally, I must say, we can't take the risk. Your magic is bound, but I might accidentally absorb it if it breaks free. It's not worth it for a simple location spell." When Noah nodded, Damian continued. "Second, and this is separate from the first, Beastie and I will use the stones' power to restore your original gifts if you wish to have them."

Noah's jaw dropped. Never in a million years would he have expected the Aether to offer to restore what his father and the Goddess had bound. Speaking of...

"'Twas a goddess who removed them. How will she react to you going behind her back to restore them?"

"You're welcome to ask her yourself, brother. Shall I call her?"

Did he want that? Or the responsibility for the type of magic the Aether's family wielded?

"Am I allowed to think on it, or do I have to make the decision this minute?"

"You have the rest of your life to decide," Damian assured him with a warm smile.

In the hours since he'd come to meet his brother, Noah was dumbfounded. The man before him was nothing like the monster he'd built up in his mind. Nothing like Damarius had made him seem when he drilled it into Noah's head to never trust Damian should he ever encounter him, cautioning him all the while on the benefits of avoidance.

"Beastie has assured me Fionola is safe for the moment. If you're still willing to join us for dinner, we'd love to have you. Vivian is a wizard in the kitchen." Damian cast GiGi a friendlier smile that spoke of familiarity. "Of course, you and Ryker are more than welcome as well."

She sauntered over to him, hips swishing to a lazy drum beat every man heard when they witnessed the dancer-like motion of her body. With a kiss on his cheek, she said, "As much as I appreciate the offer and would love to see Vivian again, I'll pass. Tonight should be about you and your family getting to learning more about your lost lamb."

She then approached Noah and patted his chest. "Take the time to truly know him," she said in a low voice. "He's worth it."

"How do you know?"

"Because he's selflessly saved my family. *Multiple* times. Damian isn't the villain you believe him to be, Noah. I promise."

And so, fifteen minutes later, he found himself seated at a table on Ravenwood's terrace, drink in hand, as he watched Sabrina run around, making leaf dragons that danced on the wind.

His heart ached as the sound of her laughter drifted to him. How many family dinners had he missed because of the suspicion and sibling resentment instilled by his father?

"She's a handful," Vivian told Noah with a laughing look for her husband. "Damian swears she gets her mischievous personality traits from me, but I beg to differ."

"I was an angel. Ask Nathanial the next time we see him."

Noah's head swiveled to stare at his brother. "The man is still alive? How is it possible?"

"He was one of two Guardians assigned to watch over the garden. When Mother woke, a battle ensued, and we lost Nathanial. Not long after, Evie, his wife and the second Guardian, crossed into the Otherworld." Damian gave him a half smile. "From time to time, when needed, Nathanial and Evie cross the veil to help us out. With Isis's permission of course."

"Sure, and my puir brain is full to bursting with all the knowledge it consumed today," Noah muttered. "Do you not blame her for your foster father's death?"

Damian shifted his head, facing the neighboring property, where the garden resided, not visible from where they currently sat. "I never had the chance to ask her if it all played out the way her visions told her it would. Nathanial, Evie, and Sabrina helped me to see it wasn't Mother's fault. The Darkness was to blame, and she mistakenly believed she could contain it for a while."

"How do you know it's gone?"

Those worldly obsidian eyes, so like his own, turned on Noah, solemn but honest. "Because I'd be destroying the world if it wasn't."

Heart pounding hard enough to leave his chest, Noah could only stare.

"You said our father claimed I held the Darkness, but I didn't. Not until it was time to deliver it to the Netherworld and leave it there in its entirety." Damian toasted him with a wry smile. "If even a speck remained, it would've consumed me by now. Rest easy, Noah."

"Noah." Vivian leaned forward and placed her hand over his, waiting until she captured his full attention. "I mistakenly feared him for a while, too. It nearly cost us our marriage and Sabrina's life. Damian's is as pure a soul as you'll find."

His brother rose to his feet, bent down, and kissed his wife in a tender, lingering way that made anyone watching uncomfortable for want of the same type of relationship.

"You give me too much credit, my love. But I'll gladly accept it." The beatific grin he gave her could charm fledglings from their nests and baby bunnies from burrows. "I'm going to see if Nate is awake. It's time he met his Uncle Noah."

"Uh—I..." But what could Noah say? His brother, sister-in-law, and their darling daughter had welcomed him with open arms despite him putting on the brakes. Why argue when they refused to take no for an answer?

"I'm glad you see it our way, brother."

"You read my mind," he stated flatly. "And you've the ability to implant thoughts. Is that why I'm coming around to liking ya?"

The fecker laughed, and the sound was contagious, though Noah had no intention of joining in.

"You were the one who projected your thoughts into *my* head first, my bratty brother. I simply responded in kind. Any budding feelings of affection are your own." Damian cocked his dark head, giving him a considering look. "I believe your existing abilities have manifested in interesting ways, don't you?"

With a press of his hand on Vivian's shoulder, he left them alone.

"Damian never intrudes on the minds of those closest to him. He'd view it as a betrayal of trust," she said. "I've spent years with him and know this to be true. The exception is her." She nodded at Sabrina, who was making her way toward the terrace. "If he feels dissension in the air toward her or Nate, he'll tap in and act if it means protecting them."

"As he should." Noah agreed with the tactic. Protecting his children should be a parent's primary goal.

"Uncle Noah! Uncle Noah!" Sabrina waved as she ran up the stairs. "Did you see my dragon? Mack taught me how to make them."

"Mack?" he asked in an aside to Vivian after nodding and pasting on a grin for his niece.

"Mackenzie Thorne-Drake. Our neighbor and Sabrina's idol." Vivian's voice was droll and held no hint of jealousy for the other woman. It appeared she didn't mind that her daughter admired someone in addition to her.

"Another Thorne," he said with a shake of his head. "Feckers seem to be coming out of the bleedin' woodwork."

Vivian laughed as she rose to her feet. "I'll leave you to entertain Sabrina while I collect our supper."

"I can do that." He rose to assist her, then cast Sabrina a grin. "Sure, and we both will, yeah?"

When she placed her small hand in his and returned his grin, Noah's heart melted completely. "And did you want a bratty little brother, too, love?"

"Oh, yes! But I knew about Nate before Mama and Papa. I'm an Oracle."

"Aye, and so you've said." With a wink, he gave her hand a light tug. "How about we help your mam with the dishes now, yeah?"

"You're just like Papa."

The smile remained on his face, but just barely.

CHAPTER 19

"Try again," Fi encouraged, frustrated Patrick's magic had gone on the blink again.

"It's no good, love. We're stuck here for the time being." A devilish gleam lit his eyes. "There's naught for it but for us to pass the time shagging, I suppose."

Torn between an impatient sigh and a laugh, Fi hit him on the stomach with the back of her hand. "Feckin' behave yourself, ya scut."

"Are you the love 'em and leave 'em sort, then?" he teased.

Right when she would've responded, the hooded figure appeared by the cell door, and Fi's frustration ramped up. Acting on impulse, she grabbed the butter knife from beside her plate and threw it between the bars at their captor's back. Her heart halted its beating when the utensil didn't immediately hit him and drop to the floor, but instead sailed through his body, clanking as it landed and skidded toward the adjacent cell door.

Patrick shouted her name, reaching for her just as the figure turned and the hood fell back from his head, revealing his face. Pain caused her chest to seize, and the air see-sawed in and out of her lungs in a wheezing rattle. Panic slithered in, taking control of her mind until she thought she'd go mad.

Fi screamed.

Her response was so loud and long, it echoed off the walls, hurting her own eardrums from the shrill sound.

"No!" Fi cried as Patrick tried to embrace her and usher her away from the opening. Away from the lurking specter on the other side of the bars. "No! No! No! *No!*"

She scratched and clawed, fighting tooth and nail to be away from him. Uncontrollable sobs wracked her body as she struggled against him.

"Fi! Love! Listen to me. I can explain."

"*You!* It's been you all along!" She stared at him in horror, shifting her gaze only long enough to note the hooded figure's sorrowful face, identical to Patrick's in every way. "No! You… I… No! I gave myself to you. My body. My *heart,*" she croaked. Sobs wracked her as she beat at his chest. "No!"

"Fionola!" Tadhg's voice rang out, along with the shouts of other prisoners on the cell block. The cacophony forced her to cover her ears from the sheer volume of the noise.

Patrick's grip on her elbows was the only reason she remained standing, but his touch was unbearable, repulsive.

"Don't touch me," she screamed, batting at his hands. "Don't touch me!"

"Fi!" Tadhg cried. "You bastard! If ya hurt her, I'll fucking rip your heart out, I will!"

The sound of prison cell doors rattling reverberated through the building, shocking her at the realization they weren't electrified at all.

"You promised you wouldn't lie to me," she said, feeling pathetic upon hearing the whining tone of her voice. "You promised," she shouted, stronger this time.

She sank down and hugged her legs to her chest, dropping her face to her knees to hide from Patrick. What a fucking fool she'd been to believe him! He'd taken her in with a few sad stories and longing looks.

She was fully aware of him kneeling in front of her, and she curbed the urge to kick him in the bollocks. Common sense prevailed—barely. If he had the power to imprison them all and maintain it as he had, what could he do to her if she angered him?

"Get away from me, Patrick O'Malley, or I'll claw your lying eyes from your fat fucking head!" she warned, leaning back as far as the wall allowed. Fear might play a part, but she couldn't bear him crossing the boundaries of her personal space.

"Fi, please listen to me," he begged. Gripping his head like he feared it would explode, he implored her to listen. "Please. That isn't me. It isn't who I am in here with you. Ya have to believe I didn't know."

"Didn't know?" she scoffed. "How could you not?"

Was he trying to justify upending those victims' lives? Hers? Rage boiled inside her. What right did he have?

"I love you," he said simply, dropping his arms to his side and making no move to touch her. "Since meeting you—"

"*Jaysus!* I hate you! And I'll not believe another word you say."

When she sneered in the face of his declaration, he sat back on his heels. He looked as stricken as she'd felt moments before.

"You're a fucking liar," she snarled, forgetting her fear and caution and warming to her rant. "From the moment you answered my phone call about Tadhg, you've been lyin' to me, and it hasn't stopped. Do ya really think I'm going to believe you've suddenly had a change of heart about all of this? That you're suddenly going to let everyone here go unharmed?"

Acceptance took the place of his hurt, and it was hard to see the torment in his darkening eyes. They were a witch's tell. The darker the shade, the more upset the person.

A witch's tell.

Belatedly, it occurred to her that his irises had progressively lightened over the time they'd been here. They'd gone from a mossy green to the emerald of *Éire's* fields in the spring, as they'd grown closer.

Yet his eye color was turning to a dense forest, deeper and darker than their first meeting, revealing his upset. Was it because she'd found him out? Because he'd destroyed what she thought they were building with his sick games, shattering her heart in the process?

Like a pendulum, her emotions swept back and forth. On one side, fear for what he'd done and was capable of doing still. On the other, fury for all of it along with his lies. With her balled fist, she struck, knocking him on his arse.

Scrambling to her feet, she raced for the door, unsure how she intended to unlock it before he caught her but willing to try anyway. It swung wide before she got there, and the shock halted her in her tracks.

Was it a trick?

"It's no trick, Fionola," he said tiredly. "Sure, and you're right about everything. I'm a fucking monster."

She spun back to see him settle into the shadows with his back to the wall. As she watched, the remaining light seeped from his eyes and his corner of the cell grew dimmer than normal.

Was he doing that? Making himself disappear?

Her heartbeat was excruciatingly loud in her ears, and she almost missed his next words.

"There's a panel at the end of the corridor." He waved a hand in the general direction. "If you flip the main switch into the up position, it'll unlock all the cells at once." His dull-eyed stare was focused on the ground.

She froze where she stood, unsure if she could trust him,

and it drew his attention to her. A bitter half smile curled his lip.

"You're safe from me, love. I'll hold the monster at bay while you shut my door and use the override to open theirs. When it's done, bring your brother back, and I'll tell you how to seal mine for good, yeah?"

Her stomach flipped, and tears stung her eyes before rushing down her cheeks. Using the heels of her hands, she swiped them away.

"You mean for me to leave you here to die?" she asked incredulously. "Are ya mad?" With a shake of her head, she swore. "Of course you're mad. What the feck am I saying?"

He huffed out a tragic little laugh, as if she amused him with her ramblings, but just as quickly, his countenance hardened. "Go now, Fionola," he ordered harshly. "Get the fuck out before it takes over again."

Why was her urge to rush back to him so strong? It made her feet leaden as she lifted first one then the other to leave.

"Fi?" His tone held desperation.

She paused in the act of swinging the door closed.

"I *do* love you, Fionola Bohannon. You gave me hope," he confessed, his voice hardly audible above the deafening noise of the hollering along the corridor.

"I loved the man I thought you to be," she replied on a sob. "But you're not him. You could never be and do what you did."

Closing his eyes, he compressed his lips, and the faint movement of his Adam's apple was visible, as if he were swallowing convulsively. Finally, he nodded. "Aye. I'm not a man anyone can love."

As THE DOOR to his cell slammed shut, so did the lid on the coffin of Patrick's dead heart. If Anu was kind, she'd take him this very moment, but he'd discovered the gods and goddesses were capricious fuckers who cared nothing for the lives of humans. It wouldn't surprise him to learn the deities viewed witches as mortals viewed cockroaches: as bugs to be crushed under their boot.

The screech of unoiled hinges swinging open grated on his raw nerves, and Patrick lifted his lids in time to see Loman's victims—no, *his* victims—sprint for the exit. A few brave souls stopped long enough to spit in his cell or throw what remained of their food.

A half-eaten croissant skidded to a halt at the heel of his shoe.

Would they be so brave if they knew the door wasn't locked yet?

He didn't blame them for their disgust or rage. Hell, if the situation was reversed, he'd likely rip the goddamned door from its hinges and beat his captor with it. Their restraint showed them to be a different caliber of person than the Patrick that existed in his twisted mind.

He was no hero.

Indeed, he'd just stood beside Fi and woke to the fact he was the polar opposite of everything he believed. Everything he wanted to be. *He* was the villain in these people's story this time around. Not Loman. Not a copycat seeking to recreate what that gobshite had.

Jaysus!

The magnitude of what he'd done was sinking in, and it hurt to discover he was nothing but a sadistic devil, forcing them to revisit the trauma of their past.

Why? Why had he done it? Was it all because he needed the puzzle pieces to fit back in place? It was the only reason that made any sense.

Or it was until the truth worked its way up from the depths of his subconscious.

Patrick gasped and clutched his head.

His alter ego believed they were safer! That they'd heal if he could reconstruct what had happened to help them, make it better. If they'd found a way to escape, wouldn't they be able to take their personal power back? Regain what was lost? All they needed was the strength of faith. He'd given them all an out, but none had recognized it.

Not even him.

It appeared Tadhg had been close a time or two, but his own demons had kept him imprisoned. Had the man solved Patrick's unspoken riddle, he'd have been free days ago. Prior to Fi becoming involved. Yet he, along with the others, had preferred to wallow in pain and disillusionment rather than find a solution.

But now the tables had turned.

He was to be the prisoner again. This time for real, and rightfully so.

Fionola skidded to a halt, tugging her brother to a stop when he tried to drag her to freedom. "He wants us to seal him in, Tadhg."

"Aye, it's a fucking grand idea!" The other man's face was ruddy in his outrage, and the light of battle glowed in his blue eyes.

Shutting his, Patrick smacked the back of his head against the cinder-block wall—*hard*—repeating the gesture a second, third, and fourth time for good measure. If he beat himself bloody, would it stop the endless self-hatred? Stop the negative dialogue in his mind? Possibly end his suffering for good? Perhaps. If he were senseless, he couldn't harm anyone else with his absurd ideas.

"Stop it!" Fionola cried. *"Stop!"*

And suddenly she was there, cradling his head against her chest. He wanted to lift his arms and hold her close, but he didn't have the right. And so he pulled away and returned to bashing his defective brains against the wall.

"Please! Patrick, please don't," she sobbed, clutching him against her in an attempt to stop his self-destructive behavior. *"Please."*

"Leave him, Fi," Tadhg barked. "He's not worth even one of your tears."

"Go, Tadhg. Get out of here and find his daughter, Dubheasa. She'll know what to do."

"Fuck that! I'll not leave ya with him."

Patrick shoved her toward her brother with the last of his strength. "Listen to him," he croaked. "Listen to your brother."

"No," she replied, reaching for him again.

He frowned at the blood on her hands.

"You're bleeding, love. Why are ya bleeding? Did I do that to you?" His horror was great. "Come, I'll heal ya. Let me heal you." He extended his arm, but was swamped by a tsunami of dizziness and pitched forward. The sight of her jean-clad knee in front of his face was unexpected and surprising. As he lay there, summoning the strength to sit up, the atmosphere around them altered. Became heavy mere moments before the crackling and popping began.

"Ah, strong magic at work," he mumbled, closing his eyes. "They're breaking down my barriers, Fionola. *Like you did.*"

"Da?" Bridget's voice was low and tender, almost tearful— definitely at odds with how strident it could be when she was on a tear. "Da, I'm here with Dubheasa and Ronan. We've come to help you."

"Don't want your help." He brushed aside the sticky substance clouding his vision. Why wouldn't everyone just leave him the feck alone? All he wanted was peace. It was all he'd ever wanted from birth, along with a strong-willed but soft woman to keep him warm at night, children he could bounce on his knee and mold into decent human beings, a welcoming home, and a pint to drink now and again.

But the O'Connors, helped by Rose, had made it impossible.

They'd turned him into a warped creature who didn't know reality from nightmares. It could be argued his current reality was a nightmare, though.

Weary to his very soul, he said, "Go away. I deserve my fate."

Or tried to.

The words were slurred and disjointed.

And completely ignored.

Strong arms lifted him as if he were a featherweight.

"Careful!" Fionola cried out. "He bashed his head."

"He did, or you and your brother did?" Bridget snapped.

"There's my darling girl. Ready to defend her kin even if it means scratching another's eyes out," Patrick murmured.

"*He* did," Fi replied as if he hadn't spoken. "The blood… I tried… I tried to help." Sheer agony coated her words, and Patrick lifted his hand toward her to send her soothing energy.

Or tried to.

His arm refused to cooperate, and he frowned down at himself. Why the fuck wouldn't they work? *Useless appendages!* When he looked to her once more, prepared to assure her he was well, fucking Noah was there and ready with an embrace.

Right when Patrick believed he had no fight left, jealousy provided the energy to struggle against those holding him. Over Ronan's shoulder, he met Noah's enigmatic look. Yet the man displayed no triumph or satisfaction, and it allowed Patrick to relax again.

Fi was where she needed to be. With *whom* she needed to be to have the life she required. Not a washed-up old fool, no better than the bastard who'd set out to destroy him. If Loman's soul hadn't been obliterated by the Death Dealers, he'd certainly be somewhere laughing about Patrick's plight.

At the forefront of his cloudy mind, a thought took hold and refused to leave him; the Authority had the power to ease his suffering and send one of their Death Dealers for him. He'd welcome it, too. His soul was too weary to continue on, anyway.

"Sleep now, Paddy," Ronan said in a soothing, hypnotic voice. "You'll be grand in no time."

For the first time since they'd met, Patrick felt kindly toward the man. His eyes closed, and blissful darkness descended.

CHAPTER 20

"They should hang an out-of-order sign around the bastard's bleeding neck and call it a day," Tadhg declared.

Fionola gasped. Insta-rage rose up inside her, and if she didn't walk away, she'd murder him for his insensitive comment. He hadn't let up since the O'Malleys had arrived to bring their father home, but at least he'd had the sense not to say anything in front of Patrick's family.

Still, he had to see she cared about the man's welfare, too, right?

For hours, they'd been cloistered in the parlor of the Black Cat Inn, awaiting word of his condition. Or she was. Tadhg and Noah were unwilling to let her out of their sight for fear she'd up and disappear on them. But where would she go? Hers and Tadhg's abductor was out of commission in a room upstairs, possibly breathing his last breath.

Her heart hiccuped.

Patrick O'Malley was too vibrant to die. Yes, he was injured, but until those last few minutes in his cell, he'd displayed a warrior's will to do what must be done. Shaking her head, Fi crossed to the window and looked out over the garden. Wild herbs grew in organized clusters, and ivy climbed the side of the house visible from where she stood. Following its ascent up the wall, she stopped when she got to the third-floor window.

Patrick's room.

Or the one he used whenever he was in town, according to him. During one of their many conversations, she'd discovered he owned a flat in Galway close to the West Coast of *Éire* that he loved so much.

Would he live to see his place again?

Goddess, she hoped so!

In the hours since she'd learned he was the one responsible for reconstructing Loman's island prison, she had time to consider his actions and the motivation behind them. The only conclusion she arrived at was he wasn't a cruel man. He'd done what he did with a purpose in mind, but she'd be buggered if she knew what that was.

"Yeah, and why are they fighting so hard to save a man who'll end up dead by the Witches' Council?" her brother said, not finished heaping abuse upon Patrick's head.

"Shut the fuck up, Tadhg," Noah snapped as Fi was rushing to escape the room's heavy hate-filled atmosphere. "Or better yet, go the feck home with ya. No one asked you to remain or for your asinine commentary."

"I'm not leaving me sister here! That man's madder than a March hare!"

"He's not likely to wake anytime soon," Bridget said coldly. Apparently the raised voices had caught her notice from the kitchen, next door.

Hoping to placate her, Fi approached. "He didn't mean—"

"I feckin' did, so don't be sayin' I didn't."

"Tadhg, I swear to the Goddess, if you don't shut up and leave right now, I won't be responsible for what I do to you," she ground out through gritted teeth. "Not one more *fucking* word."

"I'd prefer you all to leave," Bridge said in a haughty tone. "When Da is better, we'll... I'll..." She appeared at a loss. Perhaps because no one knew what to do with Patrick. Soon, if they hadn't already, his victims would appeal to the Witches' Council for justice, with Tadhg among them. It wouldn't matter if his brains were scrambled or not. The Council would call for restitution in some form or another.

"He'll get better," Fi found herself saying, praying to Anu he would. "He has to," she whispered.

Noah approached her from behind and settled his hands on her shoulders. "Come, love. I'll take you home."

Any touch, other than Patrick's, was repellent, and she twisted away.

"I'm staying." When her brother protested, she dug in. "I'm staying, Tadhg. I'll not be debating the issue with the likes of you."

"You're as stubborn as the day is long. What am I to tell Mam and Da when I get back?"

"Whatever you want," she replied tiredly. "I don't rightly care now, do I?"

"You're as mad as he is!"

"Get out! Get out! Get out!" thrummed her heartbeat as a clawing sense of claustrophobia struck. Odd, how she'd not felt a second of that locked up with Patrick, but having freedom in a roomful of strife was suffocating. It didn't help that her fury for Tadhg had reached the boiling point. If she remained, it would become a bloodbath, with her brother's broken body at the center of it.

Pivoting on her heel, she ran for the staircase.

"Fi!" Noah called out, but he didn't follow. Maybe he sensed her need to get away, or perhaps it was empathy for what she'd been through, but he let her flee.

Bridget, however, was hot on her heels and overtook her in the third-floor hallway. "You're not to see him," she said. "I'm asking you to leave him be."

"I just want to make sure he's all right. Then I'll go, yeah?"

With a toss of her bright auburn hair, Bridget crossed her arms and blocked the door to his room.

"Please," Fi begged. "Please let me see him."

"The Aether is inside with Ronan and a healer." Heaving a frustrated sigh, Patrick's eldest shook her head. "He doesn't know you're here, Fionola. He doesn't recognize *any* of us."

Hope crushed, Fi nodded, but she couldn't take her eyes off the wooden door panel behind Bridget's head.

"Thank you for caring for Da." The woman's voice was strangled, as if it was difficult to offer up gratitude.

His children couldn't have known about their relationship and likely assumed she was a stranger worried about a quasi-friend. How did Fi tell them differently? Tell them, in a handful of days, she and Patrick had bonded? That they'd found something worthwhile to build a relationship on? They'd think she was as mad as Tadhg believed her to be after what Patrick had put her through.

And perhaps she was. Maybe, like Patrick, her time spent on the island had driven her over the proverbial edge and stolen her sanity. Why else would she desire to shove Bridget aside and force her way into his room merely to stroke his brow during a magical healing?

"Will you let me know when he's recovered?" She met Bridget's brilliant green eyes, noting they were duller than the first time they'd met. Unsurprising when worry was weighing her down. "Please?"

A single nod was all she received.

"I'll rent a room if that's okay."

"It's not." Bridget averted her face. "The Black Cat is full, and I've no rooms to let."

"I see."

Patrick's family wanted her gone, and if it took a lie to do it, that's what they'd do.

"When he wakes, tell him I asked about him, yeah?" She ignored the pleading in her voice. What did it matter what the others believed? If her desperation made a difference, she'd beg.

Mouth tight, Bridget nodded once and gestured toward the stairs.

Trudging down them and out the door was harder than imaginable. Yet Fi couldn't bring herself to leave altogether. Skirting the house, she traversed the alley to the back garden. Once there, she breathed deeply of the clean air, filling her lungs and holding it until she was forced to exhale again.

It wasn't peace that filled her, but something did. Maybe it was a purpose. If there wasn't a bed in the house, fine, but she wasn't leaving until he was whole again. She was a witch with basic skills and the ability to amp up her body heat if needed. What was a little damp air compared to what Patrick was suffering on her behalf?

She staggered.

The realization was a dagger to the heart. He'd injured himself because she left him. She'd pushed and picked at him until he unraveled. Why? Why couldn't she accept him the way he was, bent mind and all? Was the hooded figure's appearance purposeful? To scare her away from peering down the hallway, or was it a cry for help?

She'd rejected Patrick's truth. Rejected him. Was it worth taking the light from his beautiful jeweled eyes? It didn't feel like it. Not now. Not knowing he was up there, suffering in pain and unaware those who loved him most were waiting for him to recover.

"I'm sorry, Patrick," she whispered. "I'm sorry I was such a miserable cow to ya."

Why was it that it took him hurting himself for her to see the truth? Maybe because she'd hours to think after he'd revealed himself and not seconds like in the cell. But at some point, in all her musings, it had occurred to her that he wasn't a monster. Mentally unstable, yes, but not evil in the way Loman had been.

She needed to truly listen to him this time if he woke and chose to explain. Discover his reasons for doing what he did, so maybe she could forgive him and receive his forgiveness in return.

Sinking down on the bench, she began her vigil.

PATRICK WOKE TO A SHADOW-FILLED ROOM—THE one he hated at the Black Cat. He struggled to recall how he'd gotten here, but the last thing he remembered was Noah holding Fionola.

Fi.

He released a savage curse and rolled to a sitting position, mentally noting his body no longer ached as it had in recent months. And didn't that make sense? He wasn't expending all his energy to maintain an island fortress while he was sleeping.

"Take it easy," Ronan advised from a nearby club chair. With a yawn and a scratch of his chest, the man dropped his long legs on either side of the ottoman and straightened from a slouched position. "You've only just had your head put back together, Humpty Dumpty, and the Aether advised avoiding walls in the near future."

Patrick snorted. "That wasn't a well-thought-out plan, to be sure."

"What were you trying to accomplish with the brain-bashing?"

"An early demise? Seems I can't do anything right these days."

Ronan didn't chuckle as Patrick assumed he might. Instead, the man appeared troubled as he flipped on the lamp next to him. "Your family was worried for ya. Bridget was beside herself and scaring off the regulars in the pub with her black scowls and barbs. It'll be a month of Sundays before they venture back."

"She always was high-strung."

Ronan's grin flashed. "We're all afraid of her, but if you tell anyone I said so, I'll be calling ya a feckin' liar, I will."

"Who would I be telling? I'm after fearing her myself when she's in a mood."

"You seem different," Ronan noted after a minute.

"Maybe a couple of blows to the head was what I needed as a reset. Not dissimilar to one of those old dinosaur computers."

"Lucky the Aether had a clear schedule this week, or you'd be wearing a helmet and licking bakery windows until your dying day."

"Ach. That's a right powerful image." Patrick's stomach growled, and he pressed his flattened palm to his abdomen to stave off the sudden hunger.

"One of you that I've held close to me heart since your last insult," Ronan quipped.

Patrick was surprised he could laugh, but the man was amusing when he wanted to be. "How long was I out?"

"Two days and nights. This morning started the third."

Nodding, he glanced toward the window, his attention caught by movement in the garden. From the back, the person strolling toward the hedge looked like Fionola.

Fi.

Of a certainty, she wouldn't be waiting for him.

A visitor of the Black Cat, then. The surprising thing was that the grounds weren't busting at the seams with pitchfork-wielding victims and their families, all calling for his blood.

Shutting his eyes, he rubbed the heels of his hands against them.

"What happens next?" he asked.

Ronan didn't pretend ignorance. "A member of the Witches' Council arrived today. She said they'll hold an inquest when you're able to attend."

"Sure, and you mean a mock trial so they can hand down a sentence on Frankenstein's monster."

Ronan didn't respond to Patrick's dark joke.

Fi would've.

She'd have replied with a cutting quip or piled on the gallows humor.

Jaysus, he already missed her. He'd only been awake minutes, yet his arms craved the feel of her body within their embrace, and his eyes burned for want of seeing her sunny smile. To say nothing of his lifeless heart.

Pretending the woman in the distance was her, Patrick continued to observe her. He sucked in a sharp breath when she turned toward the house.

Fi.

"What the hell is she doing here?" he croaked.

Ronan frowned and followed his line of sight. "She refuses to leave until she speaks to you."

Panicked, he shook his head. What did she want? What was left to say? Did she intend to lay into him or twist the Noah-knife further by letting Patrick know she'd gone back to the ever-vigilant pub owner? No one could convince him the guy hadn't been waiting to swoop in at the first opportunity. A wise man didn't let a woman like Fi walk away if he could help it.

"Tell her to go home," Patrick demanded.

"Bridg tried, but the woman wasn't having it. She's stubborn to a fault, and everyone is taking bets on who'll win between the two of them. Bridget's favored, but my money's on *her.*" During his speech, Ronan rose and strolled to the window, and now, he nodded toward the garden. "She has a right powerful anger inside her."

"At me," Patrick replied dully.

"At everyone, I think." Ronan shrugged before turning toward the door. "I'll let the others know you're awake. Should I conjure a cuppa for you?"

"I can conjure my own food. Thanks." Patrick stopped in the act of running his hands through his hair. "I *can*, yeah? It wasn't taken away?"

"Nah. Anu had a reason for returning to you what you possess."

He was referring to the O'Malley magic and the added abilities Anu had given him when she encouraged him to help Loman's previous victims. It was doubtful what he'd done was what she had in mind when gifting him the additional power.

Pausing in his exit, silvery gaze full of sincerity, Ronan gave him a small smile. "I'm glad you're back with the living, Paddy. Remember something, will ya?"

"What's that?"

"Everyone deserves a second chance. Maybe even a third if they're a stubborn eejit like you." With a wink, he sailed out the door, closing it firmly behind him.

But Patrick had already dismissed him in favor of watching Fionola.

CHAPTER 21

Fionola paced the gardens behind the Black Cat Inn, worried about Patrick and how extensive his injury might be if it was taking him so long to recover.

All that blood!

She shuddered at the remembered sight of it gushing down his scalp. How was it possible to continuously inflict that level of damage on yourself and not stop the instant pain registered? Having accidentally banged her head a time or two, she couldn't purposely do it once to herself, much less the number of times he had.

The defeat in his expression was the worst for her to bear. To see him uncaring if he lived or died had come close to destroying her. He was so broken that day.

A sob escaped her throat, and she sucked in a handful of steadying breaths. She couldn't lose it. Not until she was certain he was well. Then, she could hide in her room and cry until her stupid eyes fell out, where no one was the wiser. Cry for all she'd thought she'd found and lost within days. Cry for Patrick, who didn't deserve the cards dealt to him.

"Fi."

Noah's deep voice washed over her, and she wanted to turn around so badly, but if she did, she knew what she'd see: caring, concern, and perhaps a little longing. Censure, for sure.

His presence had grown, because she could feel it as he approached when she never could before. He'd always had a calming air about him, but this was more, somehow. What had changed? The touch of his hand on her back was electrifying, but not in the sexual way she remembered. Side-shifting to break the contact, she faced him.

"I can't right now, Noah." She was surprised by the steel in her tone, especially when her spine felt like jelly.

"You're barely holding it together, love."

"Don't call me that!" she snapped. Would she forever think of Patrick when someone used that particular endearment? It was common enough, which meant he'd never be far from her thoughts, if that was the case.

Astonishment caused Noah's dark almond-shaped eyes to flare wide. "I've always called you that, Fi."

"Well, I don't want you to anymore, yeah?" she grumbled. "I'm not your love. Not now, not ever."

Hurt transformed his face, but in a flash, he smoothed it into a mask of indifference. One she'd witnessed countless times.

"Why do you do that?" she asked. "Hide your true feelings all the bleedin' time?"

"What good does it if I lay my heart on my sleeve for all the world to see?" he countered.

Her anger began to build. Anger on behalf of herself and all the other women who weren't mind readers.

"What good? I'll tell ya!" She punched his chest, taking gratification when he winced and raised a hand to rub the spot. "Maybe if you'd shown a little *heart*, just *once*, I wouldn't have moved on!" She socked his upper arm. "I wouldn't have been open to a relationship with another man, because I'd have been secure with *you*." With vicious intent, she kicked his shin and smiled her delight when he yowled his pain. "And I might've *listened* to you and not gone with the man who broke *my* fucking heart!"

Breathing heaving, she stared at him. Her confession stood between them, and the bitter truth of what she'd said sunk in. She'd wanted Noah to love her beyond measure, to the point she would never consider another, but he hadn't. Or maybe she hadn't loved *him* to that extent, and he'd sensed it. Although their relationship ended with very little strife, it had hurt. But it wasn't anything *near* the ache she was experiencing at the moment.

"You're right."

She blinked. "What?"

"I said you're right, Fi." Holding up his hands in surrender, he ventured closer. Once a hairsbreadth separated them, he tipped up her chin. "I should've shown you what was in my heart. I love you, Fionola. More than I've ever loved anyone or anything in my lifetime." He snorted. "And trust me when I tell ya, it's been a feckin' long one."

"You're not much older than me," she scoffed.

Amusement curled his lips. It wasn't the first time she'd received the impression he was holding back a laugh at her expense.

"Exactly how old *are* you, Noah Riley?" she demanded.

"You don't want to know."

"Aye, I do." The thumb stroking her jaw was annoying and too similar to his seduction technique of the past when he wanted to avoid a truthful answer. It floored her to realize it didn't work this time. The only man whose touch she craved was in a room upstairs, fighting for his life. And she should be with him. "But not right now. I've to see to Patrick."

Noah scowled. "That's not a good idea, lo—uh, Fi."

Hands on her hips, she glared. "And why the fuck not?"

"I've been sent to take you home."

"I'll not leave until I see Patrick is well, so go on with ya."

"Fi." The warning in his tone turned her stomach to lead.

"I'm not leaving," she said, stubborn to the last. "The O'Malleys can tell me to go all they want, sure, but I'll stay right here until Patrick tells me himself."

"It's Patrick who wants you to leave," Noah said, not unkindly. Concern for her was in every line of his beautifully sculpted face.

Belated awareness struck. His gorgeousness was another reason she might've been afraid of a future with him. She'd believed she'd truly wanted it at the time, but without a doubt, she'd have found a way to sabotage it, fearing he'd leave her eventually. And why wouldn't he? She wasn't anyone special, but him—oh, great Goddess above—he was as grand a man as she'd ever seen, and women lined up for miles looking to shag him. His pub was packed to the rafters every night with hopefuls. How could a woman ever feel secure with a man like him?

Oh, for sure, she wasn't questioning his character. When committed, Noah didn't stray. It was the others she didn't trust to not fill his pockets to the brim with jotted-down phone numbers and his head with offers.

Patrick was different. He wouldn't flirt, unknowingly giving the impression of a willing man. Indeed, his semi-permanent scowl would scare most and send the weak-willed fleeing.

And he loved her.

Her stint in the garden had made clear the truth of it. Many times, she'd replayed their last conversation, torturing herself with "what ifs." What if she'd just listened to him? Truly heard what he was trying to tell her? What if she hadn't panicked when he'd allowed a glimpse of the man behind the curtain? Could she have convinced him to release the others and saved him the self-destructive actions that brought them to this moment?

She'd like to think so.

"Are you going to ignore me, then?" Noah released a half-hearted chuckle. "Yeah, and it wouldn't be the first time," he teased.

"I'll hear it from Patrick, himself," she said, lifting her chin. Noah's visage blurred, but she received the impression of movement, right before he embraced her.

"Oh, Fionola." He sighed, and the sound was unhappy. His touch was tender as he brushed her cheek. "What's to be done about you, woman?"

A sob tore at her throat, and the next thing she knew, she was pouring her heart out to him, there on the ground beside a boxed hedge with birds chirping as if they didn't grasp the depth of her despair.

With his cheek pressed to the top of her head, Noah rocked her as she cried, rubbing circles on her back as he silently listened to her misadventures. When she was empty, she inhaled a shuddering breath. Fatigue made her lids leaden weights, and after each blink, it was difficult to lift them again.

"Rest, Fi."

"I won't leave until I see him," she argued.

"We'll stay right here, you and me. When you wake, we'll storm the castle gates, we will."

"My reluctant hero." She smiled as she laid her head on his lap. Staring up toward Patrick's bedroom window, she sighed. "He thinks he doesn't deserve love, Noah. That he's a monster for what he's done."

"Isn't he?"

The lack of snideness caused her to consider the question without prejudice. Noah hadn't asked out of spite that she could determine, merely curiosity, and perhaps to force her to contemplate her answer rather than reply in a knee-jerk way.

"I don't believe he is," she said. Movement on the other side of the glass caught her notice, and she held her breath, hoping for a glimpse of Patrick. With keen disappointment that it didn't happen, Fi pressed her lids together, hoping to ease the sting. "He's grumbly when he wants to hide his softer side. Like you." Fi patted Noah's knee, smiling when he huffed out a laugh. "But he's kind, too. He never electrified those bars, and I don't believe his intention was to hurt people. The prison was posher than most inns I've seen, and all the meals were gourmet. Like a feckin' five-star resort."

"But they were still prisoners, Fi. Abducted for the second time. Do you know how that added to their torment? The PTSD is off the charts with some of those puir bastards."

"He was tormented, too, Noah. Longer than any of them, and multiple times, to boot!" She sat up and turned a beseeching look on him. "You didn't see him when he recounted those stories to me. We had hours and hours of conversation about Loman O'Connor, that manky fucker!" Swallowing hard, she met his steady gaze. "You're likely thinking I've developed Stockholm syndrome, but I haven't. I was good and furious when I found out what he'd done, but I've had nothing but time to think and recall everything. Playing it all over and over while dissecting it."

"And you don't believe your memories are skewed? That you're recalling what you want and blocking out what you don't?" Noah asked.

"No."

How did she tell him it was in the quiet moments, the ones when they cuddled down for afternoon naps or to sleep in the evenings, that she'd felt closest to Patrick the most? The beauty of their lovemaking and the quirky humor they'd shared were life-changing for her. She'd felt truly seen and appreciated for the first time in her entire life.

"I know what he did. He fabricated an entire compound and

lied to everyone, me included. And sure, it'll take time to trust him again, but I don't think he's evil. I don't believe he hurt anyone intentionally, Noah. He was mixed up in his mind and seeking the familiar in a cold, hard world."

With a sad sigh, he patted his thigh. "Take a nap, Fi. It'll be sorted soon enough."

As Noah stroked Fi's wavy strawberry-blonde hair and tucked it behind her ear, he listened for her altered breathing to indicate she was finally asleep. He'd failed to inform her Patrick O'Malley would face the Witches' Council for his actions, preferring not to destroy her heart completely. The sentence would be death should Patrick fail to make his case.

The man had asked Noah to see her home, stating she'd need him more than ever. But as he sat here with the woman he loved to distraction, he knew he wasn't who she wanted. It mattered not that his body craved hers and his heart refused to consider another. His time with Fionola was at an end, and he'd lost his chance at a happily ever after. No matter what happened with Patrick, Fi wouldn't come home to him. She'd never be his completely. And Goddess forbid the man was put to death, because she'd be inconsolable.

Footsteps on the pebbled path caught his attention, and based on the quixotic emotions of the newcomer, it was no surprise when Patrick turned the corner. He came to a stop a foot away, and his hungry gaze swept Fi's form before settling on her relaxed visage.

The man's longing was the worst. Noah could feel it like a living thing, tingling beneath his skin and causing the hairs to stand on end. The want wasn't sexual in nature, and his desire was pure, raw yearning. Patrick O'Malley hungered for Fionola Bohannon to love him as much as he loved her. The fierce ache was heavy and constant, much like a never-ending heart attack, causing pressure in the man's chest.

Noah understood the emotion for what it was. He felt close to the same for Fi, himself.

"She won't go," he said in a low voice.

"Aye. She's a stubborn one." Patrick's voice was equally low, but his possessed a raspy quality, as if, maybe like Fi, he'd been sobbing, too.

"You've gotten to know her well, then?"

Murky green eyes met his. The color told the tale of a miserable man, but Patrick skillfully hid his emotions behind a blank mask. Only when he looked at Fionola did his adoration for her show through.

"Well enough," Patrick said gruffly. "She's too open and sweet for her own good. You'll teach her not to be so trusting, yeah?"

"I'll not be teaching her anything, old man. She's a grown woman with a mind of her own."

A half smile tugged the corner of Patrick's mouth up. "Aye, she is. But like I said before, she'll need ya, all the same." His lips firmed into a straight line. "They'll be after putting me to death tomorrow."

"I know nothing about Council business, but I've heard they're an ill-humored bunch," Noah said in agreement. Hadn't he drawn the same conclusion mere minutes before? "Do you have a representative to defend you?"

"Don't need one. I'll welcome any punishment they see fit to hand out."

"You're a fool not to fight, O'Malley." Noah shook his head and dropped his gaze to Fi. "If only so you can return to her."

"She'll not have me."

He snorted and shot an amused look the man's way. "So, you're a fool in general, then, aye?" Chuckling at Patrick's scowl, Noah shook his head. "I've been around for a couple of centuries, and as sure as I'm sitting here, wishing things were different and she loved me instead, I can tell you that the woman is mad for you." He allowed all the sincerity he could muster to hang between them. "Ones like Fionola Bohannon don't come along every day, man. If your brain has truly knitted back together, then you'll recognize it and make feckin' sure to come through the trial alive."

CHAPTER 22

Patrick let Noah's words marinate as he pulled up an uncomfortable patch of grass and watched the man continually tuck Fi's hair behind her ear in long, soothing strokes.

Part of him wanted to break the offending hand, but he no longer had the right to be jealous of their closeness. Perhaps he never did. Like a stalker, he'd watched them from upstairs. After nearly beating the living shite out of the man—much to Patrick's delight—Fi had allowed Noah to hold her as she sobbed her heart out.

From where he'd stood, Patrick imagined *he* was the root cause of all her problems and heartaches. He hoped like hell his death could give her the peace she deserved.

"She clings to you in her sleep," he observed, careful to keep his jealousy from his voice. "If you love her, you should let her know."

"Sure, and I did, but she wants you."

"And you've a mind to let me win?" Patrick's laugh was genuine, albeit a bit rusty after the last few days.

"Fuck no! But it's not like I have a choice, do I? She'll pick who she picks, and I'll not grovel like a hungry dog."

"But it's what we both are, man. Hungry dogs for her affection, aye?" He shouldn't feel an affinity for his competition, but he did. In the end, though, it was about Fi's overall happiness.

Fionola's lids lifted, and she met his gaze. Her expression was void of emotion, like his and Noah's. It was as if they all feared revealing too much to the other.

"If you want my affection so badly, why is it you told everyone who'd come out here to send me away?" she asked.

"Because I was afraid to face you," he confessed, amazed at her ability to ferret out the truth when he sought to hide it. "Afraid you were only waiting to tell me how much you despised me." Without breaking eye contact, he gestured with his head toward Noah. "Afraid you'd kick me in the bollocks like ya kicked this one's shin."

Her lips twitched as if she fought a smile. "If you made me wait longer, I likely would've."

He grinned. "Then I timed it perfectly, aye?"

The smile she'd been working on disappeared as she sat up. "You don't intend to have representation at the Council meeting?"

"Not sure what the point would be. I'm guilty, Fionola." He'd said her full first name, hoping to insert distance between them, but her grimace said she understood what he was doing. "I abducted people who'd been through hell and stuck them right back there."

"But your mind was cracked, and you're not to blame."

"If not me, who? *Who?*" He shoved away his building frustration with a heartfelt sigh. "I'm the one who hunted them down, befriended them under false pretenses, and put them back in the very cage where they'd first been terrorized. *Me*, Fi. No one else."

"You didn't know, Patrick." Her voice was achingly sweet in

her certainty. "Your mind was broken for a time, but it's healed now, yeah?"

"It's healed now," he agreed. "And someone—*me*—needs to be punished for the crimes against the witch community."

Big, fat tears rolled down her cheeks to drift off her jaw. In her angst, she hadn't registered she was crying and was startled when Noah handed her the tissues he'd conjured.

"They can't exact justice on a man who was sick to begin with," she argued.

"They can now that my mind's intact, though. The Aether saw to it when he and his Sentinels repaired the damage."

Noah sent him a sharp look, and Patrick gave him a minute head shake. He didn't blame Damian for his part. It needed to be done for him to face his eventual sentencing. His and Loman's victims would demand justice, and they'd tear apart the witch community to get it if Patrick wasn't offered to them on a silver platter.

"I'll be your representative," she declared.

"You'd make a fine one, but they'll want someone with more clout, all the same."

"Someone like me?"

All three of them turned at the sound of Ronan O'Connor's voice.

He settled on a nearby bench and rested his forearms on his thighs, clasping his hands loosely in front of him. His silvery gaze searched each of their faces before landing on Patrick's.

"It was my da who terrorized those people, and you right along with them. The man was a master manipulator and relished others' pain." The haunted look in his eyes said Ronan was one of those "others." After a long exhale, he shook his head and said, "The Council is well aware he was a right proper, sadistic bastard. And I'll reveal to everyone what my childhood was like, as will Ruairí and any other cousins I can dredge up. It turned half our family mad, and our testimony should weigh in your favor, Paddy."

"Why would you do that for me? It wasn't as if I were kind to you, son."

"Son. Me Dove will love the sound of that, she will. That's all the thanks I need."

Ronan flashed a wide smile, and Patrick could swear the sun shone brighter, flowers turned their faces to the sky, and the birds sang louder. A single glance at Fi showed her to be equally charmed. Noah frowned, causing Patrick to chuckle. Likely the man was used to being the prettiest one in the room.

"What if it doesn't work?" Fi asked, worrying her lip.

The Aether stepped from the shadows and placed a hand on Ronan's shoulder. The absence of his surprise indicated the Guardian had known the man was there.

"It will," Damian said. "Patrick will have the O'Connors' testimony, yours, and mine." He shot an inquiring glance at Noah and smiled, cementing their familial relationship in everyone's minds. After seeing the two men together, there was no doubt they were blood relatives. "My brother will testify on your behalf as well, Mr. O'Malley."

"Brother?" Fi about broke her back as she twisted to look at Noah. "For fuck's sake! Sure, and you weren't lying to me when you said you were old as dirt."

"I said no such thing, woman. I *said*, you don't want to know."

Her grin caused Patrick's heart to beat faster, such was the joy of seeing it.

"True," she replied. "But I heard you say you were around for centuries."

"Two. Two centuries, and stop making me feel ancient," he muttered with a sour look.

"And I told *you*, you turn grumbly, like Patrick, when you're trying to hide your softer side." She bumped Noah's shoulder with hers, then sent a laughing glance Patrick's way. "I've you both figured out."

His desire to sweep her up and steal her away gave him pause.

"Why are you frowning?" She shifted and positioned herself in front of him. "What was it I said wrong?"

"You didn't say anything wrong, love, and fuck anyone who ever makes you feel like you do." Clasping her hand, he brought it to his lips and kissed her knuckles. "You're perfect, Fionola Bohannon, and don't be forgetting it again, yeah?"

With a wry laugh, she grabbed his face and laid a loud, smacking kiss on his mouth. "I won't, but don't you be forgetting it whenever you're vexed with me in the future, yeah?"

"I won't." He grinned.

Lowering her voice to a whisper, she asked, "So why the frown?"

"I experienced the need to run away with you. To chain you to my bed, make love to you, and never let you leave again," he confessed, equally low. Not blinking so she could see his honesty, he said, "It scares me to feel this way, Fi. What if I act on it?"

"I'm hoping you do, but only with me. After all this is over, and you're safe, I'll expect such treatment." After giving him a saucy wink, she turned serious. "You're right to worry, but it's the worry that will keep you from acting on impulse, Patrick. You've only to have faith in yourself, and all will be well."

"After this is over, I want you to take time for yourself to make sure this"—he gestured between them—"is what you truly want. Will you do that for me, love?"

"You're talking about the future."

Her smile glowed, filling Patrick with wonder that he could feel the way he did after so short a time.

He huffed out a laugh. "Aye. So I am." Looking beyond her to where the other three men had moved to give them privacy,

Patrick shrugged. "How can I lose with them on my side?" He met her loving gaze. "And with you." Throat tight with overwhelming gratitude, he simply stared at her.

"I'm real. This is real," she assured him, sensing his uncertainty.

"Thank Christ!" Tugging her onto his lap, he wrapped a hand around the back of her neck and an arm around her waist, then dipped her backward to put her off balance. A sparkle lit her eyes and started a fire in his soul. Unable to wait another second to kiss her berry-colored lips, he dipped his head and captured her mouth.

Fi's arms circled his shoulders, and she opened under him, accepting his kiss and returning his passion twofold. This moment was made sweeter by the knowledge she'd remain beside him, would continue to care about him, despite his villainous trip to the dark side.

When he let her up, her cheeks were flushed and she was laughing her delight. "I forgot we had an audience," she whispered with a giggle.

Patrick checked over her shoulder, seeing the only one who noticed was Noah.

Guilt, or something like it, was a knife to his heart. He'd been on the other side, when Rose preferred another. Then another, and another one after that. It sucked Godzilla-sized balls to see your love with another. With a grimace, he mouthed an apology and received a sad little smile in return.

Noah faced away, and his brief words to Damian and Ronan were indistinguishable. With another quicksilver half smile, he afforded them a sharp nod and strolled in Patrick's direction. When he arrived, he reached down and helped Fi to her feet before holding out a hand to Patrick.

After they were standing face-to-face, Noah nodded. "You'll be good to her, yeah?"

"If she'll have me for the long haul, she'll be treated like a feckin' princess," he promised.

"That's all I can ask." Turning to Fionola, Noah held out his arms, bussing her forehead the instant she stepped into them. "And you, Fionola Bohannon…" His swallow was audible and fed Patrick's guilt. "You're fired. So ya best never set foot in my pub again. At least not until my broken heart has had time to heal properly."

"How long is that? Until a petite brunette walks in next week?"

"Ouch. It will take at least a fortnight, but give me twice that for my wounded pride." He laughed and ducked away when she tried to gut-punch him.

After he'd sobered, he caught her hand in his, and a long, poignant moment passed between them. *"Go lonraí an ghrian go te ar d'aghaidh*, Fionola. Know that the sun shone warm upon mine when I held you."

Taking Patrick's hand in his free one, Noah placed it over hers, entwined their fingers, and curled them under before letting them go. He grinned at the unified fist, but it failed to reach his dark eyes.

"I'm guessing this is how the Goddess planned it; the two of you fighting the world together as one. Don't take advantage of her forgiving heart, Patrick O'Malley, or you'll answer to me." With that one last warning, Noah teleported away.

Patrick maintained their connection and used it to tug her against him. "I won't," he promised, looking deep into her shimmering eyes. "I promise, love."

CHAPTER 23

"*A*re you all right, love?"

Fionola shrugged a shoulder, unsure what to say. Noah had taken it upon himself to hand her off to another, and she hated that he'd done it as a male relation of old would, handing off his unwanted spinster sister. She also hated that it was so easy for him to walk away. But how did she tell that to the man she was currently with? How did one admit to mourning another relationship they didn't really want anymore?

With a tired-sounding sigh, Patrick led her to a bench and urged her to sit beside him. "I've spent too many hours inside my head, wondering what I might've done differently to make Rose not behave as she had or to make other lovers stay," he said. "Noah left you because he believed you wanted me. But if that's not the case, Fi, you should go after him."

"It is the case, but I'm not happy with the way he..." She shook her head, grateful for Patrick's willingness to listen and understand, yet unable to voice what was in her heart. "Do you think it's possible to love more than one person at a time?" she asked hoarsely, knowing it might insult him, but needing to be open and real.

He seemed to consider the question for a time as he gazed out over the landscape. Finally, he nodded. "I do. Why else can we love more than one child? More than one sibling or parent?" His smile was tender as he looked at her. "To varying degrees, we can love many people at once, but it's acting on the urges attached to those feelings that creates a problem. I'm not interested in a relationship with a woman who doesn't want me or who wants others in addition to what I can give her."

He released her hand and stood. "I'm a one-woman man hoping for a one-man woman. Think longer on what you want and give me your answer when you're ready, yeah?"

Before he could turn away, she grabbed his wrist, rising beside him. "You already have my answer, Paddy O. I wouldn't be here in this garden if I didn't want you, and you alone." She stroked his cheek and smiled. "When you were in the throes of healing, Noah tried to comfort me, and all I could think was that any touch that wasn't yours was unpleasant."

"But you love him, yeah?"

"I do, but what I feel for you is different. Deeper somehow." She frowned, knowing she was making a *haymes* of things. "I've fallen for you, Patrick O'Malley. I don't want another, but I also don't want to be forgotten and pushed aside so easily."

He laughed, and when she scowled, he cradled her face in his hands. Leaning in, he kissed her. As he drew away, his grin was broad and his eyes twinkled. "Noah didn't put you aside easily, love. *That* was a tortured man, and only *you* couldn't see it. To the rest of us, his suffering was plain and his pain great. He won't be forgetting you, Fionola Bohannon. You're not the type of woman a man can dismiss from his mind without a lobotomy."

Tears filled her eyes, her throat closed, and her sinus passages burned with the need to cry again. Shaking her head, she swallowed down her emotional reaction. "How is it you always know how to say the perfect thing to make me feel better?"

"Maybe it's because, like Noah said, the Goddess planned for us to be together." Stroking his thumbs along her cheekbones, he nodded. "I think he must be right. How else can you be so perfect for me? How else can you embody all the exemplary traits to feed my starved soul? With you, I want to be a better man."

"You're already a good man." Rising on tiptoe, she wrapped her arms around his neck and buried her face against the corded muscles along his throat. She inhaled deeply, registering that he smelled of salty ocean breezes after a storm, when the sand had been washed clean. Her favorite scent. Smiling, she pressed her lips to his warm skin. "I think you're both right. I'll be thanking Anu when my time comes to stand before her."

"That might be sooner than you think," he murmured, drawing back and pointing to the terrace. "She's just there, with Ronan O'Connor."

Fi's jaw dropped. Never in her life had she met a deity, though she'd heard stories of them paying special attention to their favorite witches. She always assumed she'd never gain their favor.

"Sure, and I don't know what to say or how to behave," she confessed as Patrick led her toward the steps.

"Like she's royalty. Curtsy and bow your head until she gives you leave to look at her," he murmured as they approached Anu.

The Goddess was tiny, no more than five-one or two, with a build that put an hourglass to shame. Thick auburn hair, leaning toward ruby, fell freely down the entire length of her back in a plethora of corkscrew curls. Pale, alabaster skin was porcelain smooth and set off by plump lips of the deepest scarlet. The overall effect was of a stunningly beautiful yet earthy woman.

Having never curtsied a day in her life, Fi felt off balance as she attempted it. The Goddess took pity on her with a hand on her elbow, and the surge of power running through her body was like eight shots of espresso along with five energy drinks all at once. Her cells seemed to vibrate at a higher frequency, and she'd swear she saw rainbows with pots of gold and chortling leprechauns waving shillelaghs in the air.

"Wow! Your touch packs a punch," Fi told her.

The Goddess smiled, revealing straight white teeth and perfectly symmetrical dimples. She was thoroughly charming.

"Those with lesser magic feel it the most," Anu told her. "The effects will wear off soon enough."

"My Queen," Patrick intoned with a deep bow. "To what do we owe this visit?"

"You and I need to have a conversation, Patrick O'Malley."

She didn't sound remotely pleased, and Fi's heart started a painful hammering.

Ronan didn't appear surprised, but then, he never had in the short time since Fi met him. The man was a virtual giant next to the petite deity, and his protective stance cemented the fact the Fates had chosen correctly to bestow him with the powers they had.

"Shall we walk?" Patrick suggested, holding his arm out for Anu to take.

Fi started to fall in behind them, but the Goddess held up a hand. "It's privacy we're needing, Fionola Bohannon. I'll bring him back to you in due course."

After the two of them cleared the terrace, Fi turned and looked up at Ronan. "Why is she here?"

"Patrick O'Malley disobeyed her orders, and she intends to take him to task."

Her heart plummeted to the ground, and the desire to run

after Patrick was overwhelming. As if sensing this, Ronan stepped in her path.

"Don't interfere, Fi. Trust the process."

His eyes had changed from their standard sterling gray to a pale silver glow, as if he were utilizing magic in some form. A calmness settled over her, and the urge to follow and defend Patrick bled away.

"Okay," she said obediently, frowning at how her will seemed to have a mind of its own.

A small smile curled Ronan's mouth. "You'll thank me later."

"Doubtful."

"YOU FAILED," Anu said, and the displeasure in her tone caused his stomach to tighten.

"Aye."

Patrick had fucked up. There were no two ways about it. He'd been tasked with healing Loman's victims, and instead, he'd created more turmoil. He waited for her to do her worst, but she continued to stroll down the path as if they had all day.

"Punishment must be doled out, of course," the Goddess said, her tone light and conversational, and at direct odds with her fearsome declaration a moment before.

"As expected." He wanted to weep. It had taken him his entire life to find a woman like Fionola, and the chances were that his punishment would result in his death. Which meant he'd need to wait until his next lifetime and hope like hell they found each other first.

"What do you believe Ronan's punishment should be, Patrick O'Malley?"

"Whatever you see fit to hand out, beloved. I'll not venture a guess as to what you've got planned—wait! *Ronan?*" He jerked to a halt and stared at Anu. "The man's done nothing wrong."

"I charged him with your welfare and seeing to it that you carried out your mission. He failed and must be punished," she replied as if it were a forgone conclusion that the Guardian take his place for whatever she intended.

"No!"

Her dark auburn brows shot up, and her mouth compressed into a hard line, causing her dimples to wink at him. "You're very daring, Patrick O'Malley."

Jaysus! What the hell had he done? He'd gone and upset the Goddess with his impulsive reaction. There was no telling what a vexed deity would do to the annoying mortal who sassed them.

"What I meant to say was, if anyone is to be punished, it should be me, Exalted One. I'm a stubborn fecker and was like to never listen to an O'Connor. You set the man up for failure if you thought to have him watch over me."

Green eyes narrowed, she cocked her head. "You believe I purposely played games with Ronan O'Connor's life, knowing he'd fail at whatever task I assigned him? Is that what you're saying?"

Her indignation caused Patrick's sphincter to tighten and his bollocks to shrivel.

Fuck!

Even on a good day, he was terrible with words. And today wasn't a good day. It was worsening by the minute. He did the only thing he could and dropped on one knee to plead for the other man's life.

"I'm after begging you to take pity on Ronan. I'm the eejit here." He bowed his head in deference to her authority. "He's been a blessing to the O'Malley clan"—and here Patrick tried not to choke at having to defend his enemy's son—"and the Aether."

After what felt like a lifetime, she said, "Rise, my child."

With a resigned sigh, he did. Her eyes were dancing with

mischief, and a pleased smile flitted about her mouth, causing the dimples to dance in her cheeks.

"You please me. Ronan is a favorite of mine, as are your family members. I'm happy to see you willing to work together as you move forward." The gold bracelet on her wrist lit as she lifted her arm, and the ogham etchings flared with a blinding white light. When she touched his cheek, he felt the zing all the way to the soles of his feet. "There will be no trial, beloved. It will be known that you've gained my favor and that the Aether has restored your mind."

"I'm free of judgment for my crimes?" Positive he was dreaming, he blinked and surreptitiously pinched the skin of his forearm. Many times, when he wasn't certain if he was lost to memories or in a real moment, he'd injure himself in some small way. The pain always woke him to the truth.

"From the Witches' Council, yes. Restitution is still yours to make should you choose."

"How?"

Anu looked toward the terrace. "Give her up and become my consort. You'll be given untold powers. During this time, you're to visit each of Loman's victims and restore what they lost to him."

"Give up Fionola?" Every bit of air escaped his lungs and refused to be recaptured. All he could do was gasp. The weight of doing what was right versus what he desired was crushing. How did he let her go after it took so long to find her? He'd waited a bleeding lifetime.

"I don't think I can," he croaked.

Yet he'd been prepared to when he believed she loved Noah. Could he do it if she forgot he existed, knowing she was safe and happy with another? Dare he request that of Anu? Considering it was destroying his will to live, and he longed for the shadowy corner of a cell so he didn't have to think.

"The choice is yours," Anu told him with a caress of his

cheek. "You'll have until midday two days hence to let me know your answer."

In a burst of twinkling lights, she was gone, leaving him to wrap his freshly healed mind around what must be done.

Restitution.

That fucking ugly word.

CHAPTER 24

"You've been quiet since your conversation with Anu," Fi said later that night. "Do you want to discuss it?"

"No." He sipped his pint of plain and surveyed the packed pub. Lucky O'Malley's was bursting at the seems, and he was positive they were over the legal limit allowed in an establishment.

"Patrick."

Fi's low-voiced censure brought his head around, and he met her concerned expression with a grimace.

"There's naught to discuss, love. I've a choice to make, and it's not one I'm chuffed to be making."

Reaching across the table, she clasped his hand between both of hers. "And does that choice have something to do with me? Because you haven't been able to look me in the eye since speaking with Anu."

"Can we leave off arguing tonight? *Please?*" He didn't want their last two nights together to be filled with turmoil. Rather they have a few drinks, fall into bed—if only to cuddle—and part with sorrow, if it came to that, than go round about a decision he wasn't prepared to make.

Releasing him, she sat back. Disappointment and hurt were stamped on her face, and Patrick felt like a right proper bastard for causing her pain. Making an impulsive decision, he stood and downed his drink. Then, he moved to her side of the table and leaned in to kiss her.

"I love you, Fionola Bohannon, and it's my fondest wish you remember it always. But in case you forget, I'll tell you true that you'll have the number-one place in my heart for the remainder of my days and well past when I've entered the Otherworld."

"Why does this sound like goodbye?"

His heart caught in his throat, and he called on every bit of acting talent he possessed to make it appear otherwise. Gifting her with a roguish grin, he drew her to her feet and grabbed her drink.

"Come. I've something I've been meaning to do."

When they reached what served as a stage, he shooed away those in front and gestured for Fi to sit down at the abandoned table. Nerves ate at him, and he called himself ten kinds of fool for putting himself on display. He drank down the last of her pint in a single guzzle, wiped away the foam with the back of his wrist, then waved at Ruairí, indicating he should bring another.

All eyes were on him as he climbed the steps to the microphone, and Cian stopped strumming to welcome him with a grin. "You're gracing us with a song, Da?"

"I'm gracing Fionola with one, aye."

He heard her gasp over the crowd noise, but he didn't turn until he accepted the guitar from Cian. Positioning himself on the stool, he strummed as he adjusted the strings, and when he was satisfied, he met her glowing eyes across the distance.

"'Tis a song I wrote about true love," he said into the mic while he began to play.

Fi raised a hand to cover her smiling mouth and shook her head.

He nodded. "Sure, and it makes me sound like an eejit to say it, but I've loved ya from first sight, Fionola Bohannon."

In this world so wide I wandered, lost but free,
Searching for signs, a clue of what's meant to be.
Every soul I met, felt like a passing phase,
'Til you opened that door and your face my eyes gazed.

And in your eyes, I saw the spark of fate,
A light that guides me through my darkest days.
We were written in the stars, no need to explain,
In this love, we found our place.

You're my true north, my heart's compass in the storm,
Every piece of me aligns when you're in my arms.
We're fated, meant to be, forever intertwined,
In this dance of destiny, you're my heart's design.

Through the stormy nights and the endless tries,
You're the melody that makes my spirit rise.
Every beat of time has led me to you,
In this endless dream, we're painting skies so blue.

And in your touch, I feel echoes of the past,
A love we built, meant forever to last.
You're my forever, my destiny so true,
In this love, I've found my way to you.

You're my true north, my heart's compass in the storm,
Every piece of me aligns when you're in my arms.

We're fated, meant to be, forever intertwined,
In this dance of destiny, you're my heart's design.

And in this tapestry of life, we're a thread so fine,
Weaving dreams and love through the fabric of time.

The last note faded, and the pub remained silent for the count of five—just long enough for him to set aside Cian's guitar and stand—before the roar of approval and deafening applause began, led by Fi. She jumped to her feet and ran up the steps to meet him halfway, leaping into his waiting arms. Drawing his mouth down to hers, she kissed him like a hero coming home from war, and nothing had tasted so sweet as her love pouring into him.

How was he ever supposed to give her up? Give this up? He'd go mad in no time. Tears burned the backs of his lids, and he kept his eyes closed as he held onto her like a lifeline.

"Let's go," she said, dragging him toward the exit. "I want to spend the rest of the night alone with you." The twinkle in her eyes was naughty to the extreme, and Patrick had never seen a more welcoming sight. "Maybe I can inspire another song. A bawdy one, next time."

"Sure, and I've written those for you, too."

Her laughter was a thing of beauty, lighting her face and making everyone who'd heard it smile, despite not having been in on the joke.

They'd made it to the alley sandwiched between the Black Cat Inn and Lucky O'Malley's when a hulking figure stepped into their path. Although surprised, Patrick's reaction was instinctual, and he tucked Fi behind him.

"Are you lost, man?" he asked.

"No."

The stranger's vibe was menacing, and there was little doubt he was seeking trouble.

"Fi, go back into Lucky's," Patrick ordered.

"No, Pat—"

A scream choked off her refusal, and he spun to help her.

Too late.

Another man had her by the hair with a knife to her throat.

"Take it easy, man," Patrick said with a calmness he didn't feel. "Whatever you want, I'll give it to ya, but you'll be letting her go first."

"She's what we want." The second assailants' eyes were small and cruel, as if he thrived on causing his victims' pain.

Patrick was familiar with his sort. Hadn't he dealt with Loman O'Connor and the bastard's sadistic brothers?

"If you're thinking to harm her, you won't survive the night," he warned, infusing steel in his tone.

"You're owed for the trouble you caused, and she'll serve right enough," the brute behind him said.

"And I intend to pay, but she's innocent, like whoever it was I wronged."

Fi's eyes flared wide, and it was the only warning he received about the oncoming attack. Sidestepping, he pivoted and gripped the man's wrist, giving it a vicious twist until the knife in his grasp clattered to the cobblestones.

With a sweeping kick, he sent the blade into the darkness right before ruthlessly breaking the man's forearm and sending a fist into his temple to take him down.

"Your companion's in for a long nap, and you're next, ya fuck," Patrick growled.

The tip of the beady-eyed assailant's weapon was pressed to Fi's throat, close to the carotid artery. If the man decided to stick her, she'd bleed out before Patrick could dispatch him and get to her.

But he'd die trying.

His intent to kill was plain to see, and the thug's expression turned uneasy.

The knife he was holding against Fi's unblemished skin lowered a few inches. "Don't know who you wronged, but we were paid by the lady to—"

A shot rang out.

With a gurgle, the man dropped to the ground to stare sightlessly at the clear night sky.

"If you want something done right, you have to do it yourself, ya do," a female remarked from the shadows.

"Rose."

Jaysus! The hits kept coming.

"I'd thought you dead by Loman's hand," Patrick said as casually as he could manage.

More's the pity that she wasn't. All his searching had turned up naught, and he'd gone off the assumption she didn't make it off the island or that she was too clever to ever show her face around here again. But of course it tracked that she'd be the one to hire assassins to make his life a continued misery.

"Sure, and I thought the same of you," she replied without expression as she did a visual sweep of Fionola's person. Smirking, she lifted a dark brow, and Patrick never wanted to smack the smugness from her beautiful face as much as he did at that moment. But he wasn't Loman, and he didn't hurt women.

But you did, his conscience taunted. *You locked them up and threw away the key, all for the sake of your peace of mind.*

Yeah, his choice wasn't one at all. He had restitution to pay, and he expected it started now if Karma had her way.

As Rose sauntered forward, he did, too, carefully positioning himself in front of Fi, who'd remained unnaturally quiet since his ex-wife shot the hired henchman.

"I heard your caterwauling, Paddy. It's an embarrassment to the O'Malley name, it is." Rose gestured toward the pub with her gun, and then frowned at the weapon as if she were surprised she still held it.

"I never claimed to be a rock star."

Fi's hand settled on his mid back, and a bit of the tension in his shoulders eased. At least one person appreciated his gesture.

"Why are you here, Rose?" With a nod to the dead man at his feet, he shook his head. "What's this all about? Are you not done torturing me, then?"

"I came to apologize for my part in Dubheasa's death and saw these two milling about." Turning the gun so the grip faced him, she held it out. "I want no more hate between us, Paddy."

And he'd be buggered if she didn't appear sincere, but he also knew she couldn't be trusted. He mentally viewed their situation from all angles, hoping to discover the trick. Nothing came to mind. No reason for her to turn the tables and play the ally.

Accepting the gun and praying it didn't magically explode in his face, he said, "Then ya shouldn't be insulting a man's singing."

She laughed, and it transformed her face from simply gorgeous to stunning. Not for the first time, he wondered what she ever saw in him. He'd been a fool to believe he could hold on to a rare butterfly like her, and since meeting Fi, he understood a femme fatale the likes of Rose had never been for him. The thing he desired most was a simple life with a woman who truly loved him and was willing to share in that life he wanted so fecking badly.

"In case you didn't notice, these two didn't possess magic," Rose said. "You'll need to call the *Garda* to sort this mess out in place of the Witches' Council."

"Better for you, yeah?" he couldn't resist taunting.

Rose simply smiled as if his comment was expected.

"Will you be sticking around to make a statement?" Fi asked her, moving to stand beside Patrick.

"Aye."

"They said a woman hired them," he felt compelled to add. "I'm sure you know nothing about that, yeah?"

"It wasn't me, Paddy. I heard that one say it, but I swear on my life it wasn't me."

"I believe her." Fi grimaced, and she watched Rose like a hawk watches a field mouse. "I might be a feckin' fool for it, but I do."

He did, too. Rose hadn't displayed a single one of her standard tells.

"That leaves you with an unknown enemy, Paddy," Rose said, and her concern appeared genuine. Her caring was discombobulating. "A dangerous one."

CHAPTER 25

Their group spent the remainder of the night speaking to the *Garda*. After the tents were erected, the bodies bagged, and the onlookers shooed away, Rose, Fi, and Patrick were separated so their individual statements could be taken. With regret on his visage, one of the officers confiscated the gun and took Rose away.

Patrick would be surprised if they ever made it to the station. His ex-wife had the ability to influence malleable young men like the one who had detained her for the shooting, and she'd come out of this mess smelling like the flower she was named for.

On leaden feet, he escorted Fi up the stairs to his bedroom, where she proceeded to cuddle against him and fall into a slumber. Yet for him, sleep was elusive.

Who wanted them dead?

Dawn came and went, and Fi slept on as he mulled over potential threats. The only conclusion he drew was a victim's family member. But why not come after him themselves? Why hire non-magical assassins to do their dirty work? Surely they had to know they stood no chance against a warlock with his abilities.

A knock sounded at the door. Other than to snort softly and snuggle down, Fi remained sleeping as Patrick eased from beneath her body to answer.

Grim faced, Dubheasa pulled him into the hall. "We've not found the woman responsible."

"Did you think it would be so easy, then, love?" He grinned in the face of her ire and drew her to him for a tight hug.

"I'm frustrated, Da. Who has the ability to hide from a pair of Guardians?"

"A deity, Aether, or other Guardians?"

"Aye, and we know it's not Damian, Ronan, or me. So why would any god or goddess wish to harm you?"

"I don't know. It may just be someone we haven't considered, or we haven't looked in the right direction yet. But it won't matter after today."

The door behind him swung wide, and Fi, looking delightfully rumpled, scowled. "You'd best be telling me what's happening today, Patrick O'Malley, or whoever's after you will need to stand in line to bash you over the feckin' head."

Dubheasa, the traitor, laughed.

"Yeah, and I intended to tell you this morning, but you were sawing logs like a lumberjack," Patrick retorted as he drew Fi's hair back and dropped lingering kisses along the column of her neck. With no little satisfaction, he noted she craned her neck, allowing him full access.

"I'll give ya a lumberjack," she muttered, but her fingers curled around his shoulders as she clung to him. "And about three hours to stop your seduction."

He chuckled and released her.

Blue eyes glinting with humor, she shook her head. "What are you up to, Patrick O'Malley? And know I didn't come out of me mother's womb yesterday, yeah?"

With a shudder that wasn't all that fake, he scowled. "Please don't ever mention Clara's womb again when I'm feeling frisky. The visual will kill my drive for a fortnight or two."

"Fair enough." She shared a grin with Dubheasa. "Can I beg you for a cuppa, then we can get this discussion started proper like?"

"Bridget has breakfast waiting, but she's not happy you and Da slept the day away."

Fi thread her arm through Patrick's and gave him a squeeze. "I did all the sleeping. Your da stayed awake to worry."

"You knew about that?" He was surprised she noticed, but he shouldn't have been. Fionola was as observant a person as he'd ever met. Perhaps he should've discussed the possibilities of their enemy with her.

"Aye. Whenever I woke, you were staring into space. Part of me feared you'd gone back to the island, in your mind."

Her comment chilled him. Was that always going to be a worry for them both?

"His neurotransmitters were fully healed, Fi," Dubheasa said, not unkindly. "Neither of you will have to stress over a relapse again."

Patrick released a breath he hadn't been aware of holding. The assurance was welcome, indeed.

When they entered the kitchen, Bridget was her usually busy self, but Ruairí inserted himself at every opportunity, attempting to ease her workload.

"As much as it pains me to sing the praises of an O'Connor, you're likely to never find a better mate than the one you've got, Bridget, me love," Patrick said with a hard pat on Ruairí's back. "He sees you, and that's half the battle in the fight for a lasting relationship."

Her laughing eyes met those of her lover, and she winked. "Da's coming around."

"Should we celebrate this day with a drink?" Ruairí asked with a chuckle.

"I'll settle for a coffee with a dram of whiskey," Patrick replied as he reached for two mugs. "Fi?"

"Tea."

"She's the reasonable one, she is." He gave her a wink and set the kettle to boil before pouring himself a cup of coffee from the carafe. "Who are we waiting on, regarding this discussion?"

"The boys." Bridget piled beans, eggs, tomatoes, sausage, and potatoes onto two plates. "Toast is on the table with the jam," she said as she handed him the full dishes and nodded toward a seat. "I'll make your coffee, Da."

"You don't have to wait on me, love. I've two capable hands, yeah?" Patrick kissed her cheek and shifted out of the way to allow Carrick's wife entry to the kitchen.

"Yeah, Da, but I've been doing this so long, it would throw off my entire day if I were to pass off the work to another."

"Believe her," Roisin said as she gathered two mugs in one hand and the carafe in the other. After placing them on the table, she took a seat on the bench with her back to the wall. "Carrick's on his way, after he sees Aeden off to school."

"Should we move to the pub, if more people are joining us?" Fi asked, eyeing the size of the room.

Chuckling, Patrick pulled her to her feet, sat in her seat, then drew her back down onto his lap. "There's plenty of room, love."

Face flushed, she laughed and crammed a slice of toast in his mouth. "Only if every couple doubles up like us."

He grinned around the bite, then noticed the silence around them. As he used his drink to wash down his food, he raised his brows. "What?"

"It's good to see you happy, Da," Dubheasa said with a soft smile.

Heat crept up his neck, and it suddenly became difficult to meet anyone's eyes. Being the center of attention wasn't something he particularly cared for, and last night's performance for Fi had been born from his need to tell her how much he loved her. But all of it would disappear.

Soon.

The bustle in the kitchen resumed, and when he glanced up from his plate, it was to find Fi watching him.

"What aren't you telling me?" she asked in a quiet voice.

"Now's not the time, love. But I promise to tell ya true when it is. Can that be good enough for ya?"

She considered it for a long minute before nodding. "Aye."

By the time the rest of the O'Malleys and their significant others arrived, it was determined they should use the private meeting room at the pub to house everyone. Ten people in the kitchen created a claustrophobic atmosphere for Fi, and thankfully, Patrick recognized her stress. Or perhaps he needed more room himself, after his incarceration on the island. Her own confinement had triggered a newfound desire for open floor plans.

"You all right, love?" he asked after they settled onto their seats.

"Aye."

After a squeeze of her hand, he released her and focused on Ronan. Wariness was in his eyes whenever he looked at the other man, and Fi wondered if it would always be so. She hoped not. It would make for awkward family functions if he didn't learn to trust the Guardian.

"Does he look so much like him, then?" she leaned forward to ask.

"No. It's the power he wields that's the problem." Patrick's mouth curled down, and he shook himself. "I've no reason to hold his da's actions against him, but it's a hard habit to break."

She could easily understand why he'd feel that way, considering what he'd told her. For over two hundred and fifty years, the O'Malleys and O'Connors were at war. Longer than that, if one considered their feud began before the powerful sword that brought about the suspension of the O'Malleys' magic was stolen. Only a few of the newer generation wanted the fighting to end, but as a man conditioned to look for betrayal at every turn, Patrick would have a difficult time putting his fear and suspicion aside.

"For what it's worth, it appears both Ruairí and Ronan love their mates," she told him. "My understanding is that both men have sacrificed for your daughters more than once."

"Aye." Patrick's expression was strained, pinching the lines around his eyes and mouth. "I'll come around."

"I wish I could make it better for you." Gracing him with a tender smile, she brushed her fingertips along his wrist. "All will be well, Paddy O."

His lips twitched as his eyes warmed, and it pleased her to see his irises were lighter. Still, there was something holding him back, because they hadn't reached the emerald color she'd witnessed during his happiest state. She only wished she knew what that something was because she wanted desperately to fix it.

Dubheasa called the meeting to order once Eoin and Brenna arrived. Trailing them was a man named Fintan Sullivan, who Bridget informed her was a cousin to Brenna and a Seer, to boot. Their connection was apparent in the multicolored hair they both sported, along with their strong features. Brenna's face was softer, more rounded, but her large eyes were shaped the same.

When Fintan's sea-foam-colored gaze repeatedly strayed to Fi, she shivered. A sneaky feeling wouldn't leave her, and she was positive he knew things about her that she'd never told another. The second she had more time, she intended to discover what a Seer could actually do.

"Rose swears it wasn't her who hired the men, and for the first time in my life, I believe her," Patrick was saying when Fi tuned in to the conversation.

She nodded. "I got the same impression. If she knew who they were, she's the best feckin' actress I've seen."

"So not her," Bridget said as though she were disappointed by the fact. "Did the brute wake up yet, or is he still out?"

She referred to the man Patrick had punched in the temple. The guy had slipped into an unexplained coma and hadn't woken as of this morning, according to Cian.

"We can wake him with a simple spell," Piper said. Until now, she'd been listening with interest but refraining from contributing to the conversation. "I'll call my cousin Alastair and see if he'll help me while the rest of you spread your resources and look for our mystery woman."

Brenna turned to her cousin. "Have you received anything from the ancestors, Fin?"

Although he answered in the negative, his frown indicated he had. Once again his gaze locked on Fi, and she understood he was holding back because of her. "If you'll excuse me, I've a call to make."

She rose and pressed a hand to Patrick's shoulder, then left the room. When she was clear of the others, she dialed her mother.

"Fionola?" Mam's tearful voice fed Fi's guilt for not returning home immediately after escaping from the prison. She didn't trust Tadhg to represent what happened or her desire to stay with Patrick until he was recovered.

"Hi, Mam," she said, equally as tearful.

What was it about the unconditional love of a parent that always made a grown woman feel like a child? Her mother was as strong and dependable as they came, but if she was in such emotional state, her fear must be great.

"When are you coming home? Tadhg said you stayed with that awful man. Why would you do such a thing, girl?"

"He's not awful, Mam. Sure, and he was confused for a bit, but he's healed now."

Clara rattled off a few choice phrases, and Fi winced at the things coming from the other side of the call. Tadhg added his vitriol in the background, feeding into their mother's worry.

Infusing authority into her voice, Fi said, "Mam, calm down and stop letting Tadhg rile ya. Patrick is a good man, and I'll not have you saying such things about him."

A snort sounded behind her and caused her to turn. The man in question sat atop a bar stool on stage, in his hands was a guitar, and he was fiddling with the tuning pegs. Amusement curled his lips, and his eyes were laughing when they met hers.

With a glare, she stalked to the opposite end of the pub. The first notes of the song he wrote drifted to her, and Fi's heart melted as she recalled the words he'd sung the night before.

"I have to go, Mam. I just wanted you to know I'm okay, yeah?"

"When will you be home?"

"Soon."

"Tell her you'll be home tomorrow," Patrick called out.

She frowned across the distance. How had he heard the question, and why did he sound so positive? Did he intend to send her packing? He had another think coming if he believed he could get rid of her so easily.

"Soon," she said again, firmer this time. "I'll phone you tomorrow and check in. You're not to worry, all the same."

"You should go home, Fionola," he told her the moment she ended the call. "It's safer."

"Shut your gob, Patrick O'Malley! I'll not run because some mad cow is after ya."

"Is it your intent to always be this bossy?"

"Are you man enough to handle it?" she challenged him as she ascended the stairs.

Setting aside the guitar, he crooked his finger, beckoning her nearer. When she stopped in front of him, fists on hips and the light of battle in her eyes, he grinned and hauled her close.

"Likely I'm not, but I'll die a happy man from trying."

CHAPTER 26

In the quiet shadows of the sleeping pub, Fintan Sullivan observed the kissing couple. They were about to face another hurdle, and soon, unless he missed his guess. He'd come out to speak with Fionola, only to find her on the phone and Patrick hanging about like a damned wraith, unwilling to let the woman out of his sight. The overprotectiveness made Fin frown harder, because he'd a vision of the man walking away from her for good, though it wasn't clear precisely why yet. The Sullivan ancestors were stingy with their visions at times.

When Fionola pulled back, the bright glow of love lit her aura. Even had he not been able to see such things, Fintan would've known she was smitten by the flush of her cheeks and the sparkle in her large blue eyes. He hated to be the one to tell her about her upcoming heartache, but he didn't want her to be blindsided by someone she trusted. Being on the receiving end of betrayal hurt like a motherfucker.

As if sensing his presence, she cast a side glance his way. Her smile dimmed, and she murmured something to Patrick, who turned to look at him.

"What's the craic, man?" he called out to Fintan.

"I've a mind to speak to Fionola."

After a quick study of his serious face, Patrick slowly, as if reluctant to, dropped his hands from her hips and rose. The couple shared another sweet kiss before parting, with Patrick heading out the door and Fionola joining Fintan.

"What's this about?" she asked curiously. "Does it have something to do with what you saw during the meeting, then?"

A smile curled his lips. "Noticed that, did ya?"

"Aye."

Hesitant to say, he looked toward the door Patrick exited. "Where's your man gone?"

"Don't know. He mentioned giving us privacy and that he'd a thing to do. Should I be worried?"

"I think you should seek out Noah Riley and ask him what he knows about yesterday's attack."

She sucked in a breath so sharp she coughed, and Fintan experienced a twang of remorse for his bluntness. "Ach, and I'm after apologizing for being as dull as a turnip. I didn't mean he's responsible, just that he likely knows who is. Or he will by the time you go see him."

"Why can't you just tell me?"

"Sure, and that's a grand question, but not one I can answer easily enough." He exhaled a frustrated sigh. For years, he wondered the same bleeding thing. His life would be a helluva lot easier if he could just blurt out what he knew and be done with it. Subtle nuances were not for the likes of him! "My ancestors aren't inclined to be forthcoming. Their greatest pleasure is forcing me to run around like a feckin' chicken without its bleedin' head."

Her mouth twitched, and humor lit her eyes. "My sympathies."

They conversed for a short while, mainly because she had questions about his gifts and he had the time to humor her. Yet as he turned to go, the sensation he associated with an incoming vision struck. His nerve endings tingled, and his brain felt too tight for his skull. The room disappeared, leaving him in a weightless state in an endless black space with no sense of up or down. He didn't have time to wonder what Fionola thought of his reaction, but he'd been told in the past that his eyes tended toward an opaque white and went sightless. All in all, an unnerving thing for an onlooker to see. It also left him vulnerable to attack, should someone take it into their mind to strike, and he hated it.

"Fintan."

Experience had taught him the omnipresent voice was a collective of his ancestors, with the dominant member's message taking precedence over the others. He didn't bother to answer. There was no point. They'd reveal what was necessary and throw him back like an unwanted catch from a fisherman, leaving him to flounder and attempt to get his bearings.

"Save the patriarch."

"What pat—"

He was thrust back into the land of the living, and he staggered, unprepared for such a short encounter.

Although Fionola stared at him in abject horror, she instinctively caught and helped to steady him.

"Thanks," he growled, not irritated with her, but the entire situation. Why couldn't he be at the Sullivan estate, ensconced in the library with a good book, away from the world at large?

"You didn't finish your question."

He frowned, trying to recall what he'd asked her. Nothing came to mind.

"You said, 'what pat,' then swayed on your feet," she prodded gently.

"Oh! Aye. Yeah, and that wasn't for you—" But it was, he recalled with sudden clarity.

Patrick O'Malley was the patriarch!

Fuck!

"Where did your man go?" he demanded briskly. "And don't be plaguing me with twenty questions. Tell me and be done with it, yeah?"

Goddess love her for recovering from his salty attitude as quickly as she did, because Fi shook off her surprise and pointed toward the neighboring building. "Black Cat Inn. Said he had an errand." Her head whipped in the direction she pointed, and she swore under her breath. "Let's go!"

They took off at a run, and by the time they arrived at Patrick's room, he was gone.

FIONOLA SURVEYED the pin-neat space and immediately registered that Patrick had cleared out. A quick check proved his toiletries were missing from the bathroom and the wardrobe contained no clothing. The linens and comforter had been stripped from the bed and were placed in a neat pile beside the door.

"He left me!" she exclaimed aloud in her shock. How could someone kiss her as he had, then leave immediately after? No hint he was going or a goodbye and good riddance. Just disappeared without a word, and her thinking they had developed something special after his beautiful song. She turned stricken eyes to Fintan and winced at his compassionate expression. For a hardened man like the Seer to show his softer side, he had to believe she was a pitiful sack.

Her anger built.

"What did you want with the fecker, anyway?" she snarled.

"I'm to 'save the patriarch.' That means Patrick O'Malley."

"You'll be needing to save the bastard, all right. When I find him, I'll make his time with Loman O'Connor look like a bleedin' picnic, I will!"

Fintan's dark blond brows shot up, and he sputtered a laugh. "Scarlet in your mam for the way you turned on your mate just now!"

"Did you miss the kissing and flirting, then?" she asked incredulous that he didn't see it from her side.

"Aye, but I also saw the crafty expression on his mug. Though I'd say *you* seemed to miss it with all the stars in your eyes."

She narrowed those eyes on Fintan. "Just tell me what you know and be done with it."

"I'm ashamed to say I'm after fearing ya, I am."

"You're nothing of the sort, man. And if I have to ask ya again, I'll be calling Bridget in here to take you to task, yeah?"

"I told you what I know," he said as if he were talking to an eejit of the first order. "You're to find Noah Riley to learn what he's uncovered, and I'm to save the patriarch. That's all me fuckin' ancestors revealed, and don't think I'm chuffed about it."

"Fine!" She shut her eyes, prepared to teleport, when his fingers closed around her wrist. "What the bleedin' hell—"

After glaring her ire, she gave his hand a pointed look.

"I'm going with ya," he replied, fatigue heavy in his voice. "Did I not just say—"

"Yeah, yeah, yeah! Hold on."

Closing her eyes again, she envisioned Noah's flat above the pub. From deep within her cells, she gathered her standard store of magic and shaped it into a thread. It would be invisible to the naked eye, but it allowed her to determine if anyone or anything was in the way of her teleport. It could ruin a witch's day to stumble upon Noah in the middle of bow chicka wow wow.

She retrieved the thread when she received the all clear and, once again, envisioned the space as she knew it to be laid out.

Her body warmed past the point of uncomfortable, but quickly cooled the instant she landed on the other side.

Snapping her lids open, she noted the curiosity on Fintan's countenance. He nodded as if the flat was as he expected it to be, then led the way to the door. They thundered down the stairs, not bothering to be quiet. No one would ever hear them over the roar from the taproom.

As they rounded the corner, Noah appeared and stepped into her path, causing her to impact his chest and knocking them both backwards a few feet.

"Jaysus!"

"Noah! Just the man I was looking for." She latched onto his wrist and dragged him toward his office. "No time to waste!"

"What the fuck is going on? And who the fuck are *you*?"

CHAPTER 27

"You don't know me?" Fi asked in horrified wonder. How was it possible Noah had lost his memory of her?

"Of course, I know you. For feck's sake, Fi! The wards I have in place upstairs wouldn't let just anyone in." He scowled and gestured to Fintan with his thumb. "I'm asking who the fuck he is, and why were you coming from my flat?"

"Oh!" She waved away the question and resumed dragging him toward the office. "I'll explain in due time, to be sure, but let's go where we can hear ourselves think."

Once they were situated, with the door shut, Noah indicated they sit down, and perched on the edge of his antique wood desk. The beast consumed half the room, leaving little remaining area for visitors or comfort. He either didn't notice or didn't care, as he regarded them from his elevated position.

"What's going on, Fi? What's with the drama?"

"According to the Seer here, you know something I don't, and we're to save the patriarch, which happens to be Patrick."

"Ah." A world of understanding colored his beautifully sculpted face, and he shifted his attention to Fintan. "A Seer.

I've only met one in my life, name of Sullivan. You know of him?"

"My uncle, but he's pushing up daisies and has been for a quarter of a century. Name's Fintan Sullivan, and I've taken his place."

Noah nodded. "Can ya provide any clarification?"

"Not yet. Other than you've overheard something, but you may not know what it is ya heard."

Black brows drew together over midnight-colored eyes as he considered Fintan's words.

"Last night, Patrick and I were attacked by two non-witches in the alley between his house," Fi said.

"Jaysus!" Noah's expression declared he was ready to rip the villains limb from limb. "Tell me O'Malley dispatched them, or give me their direction."

"Sure, and it was his ex-wife who shot the man with the knife to my throat."

He paled. His focus dropped to her neck, and he exhaled forcefully when he registered the lack of injury. "So his wife returned, shot the man, and miraculously refrained from getting even with O'Malley, even though you, his latest lover, were present?"

"It's not like that. She doesn't care that he's moved on, but was a right proper bitch to him in the past, and unfaithful, to boot!"

"Sure, but in that case, why *wouldn't* she take delight in his demise?"

Fi shrugged. "Don't know, don't care. Everyone is convinced she's innocent of hiring the men."

"Why did anyone believe it was her to begin with?"

"The man mentioned he was paid by a lady. But he never finished telling us who before Rose shut him up for good."

"And you still don't think she did it?" he asked with a laugh.

"No." Maybe she was a fool, but she believed Rose. More

importantly, she believed Patrick believed her, which was saying a lot, considering he didn't trust many.

"A woman, huh? Is that what you believe, too?" he asked Fintan. When the Seer confirmed it, Noah's gaze grew thoughtful. As he considered what was said, he looked toward the door as if mentally recalling things he'd seen or heard. Seeming to reach a conclusion, he climbed to his feet and held out a hand to assist Fi up.

"We've a need to see your mother, love."

"Mam? What does she have to do with this?" Unease unfurled in her stomach.

"Everything." His expression was grim.

Not wanting to believe her family was in any way involved, Fi looked to Fintan, but he nodded.

"So now you know what's about to happen when you didn't five minutes ago?" she asked dryly.

His grin was sheepish.

"You're right about your feckin' ancestors, and you can tell 'em I said so." She smiled when he chuckled, then leaned in for a brief hug. "Thank you, Fintan."

"I'll be going with you in case you've need of me," he reassured her.

They followed Noah out the door and down the hallway into the pub. When Fi saw the gathered crowd, she hissed out a breath and touched his arm to get his attention.

"It's too busy for you to leave. We can go," she said in a raised voice to be heard above the crowd.

He drew her back into the hallway and leaned closer so she could hear. "I don't give a shite about any of those people. They can all bugger off." Sandwiching her face between his palms, he graced her with a look so tender her old self—the woman who'd once adored him—wept inside. "Let's go find Patrick."

Overcome by his willingness to help despite her choosing another, her chest tightened, and she could only nod. He clasped her hand and tugged her through the pub, pointedly ignoring anyone who hollered his name. Before they exited, he drew Marta aside. "You're in charge for the foreseeable future. Don't fuck it up."

The cheery, blonde-haired beauty rolled her sky-blue eyes and winked at Fi. "His managerial skills are top-notch, they are!" With a dismissive wave in Noah's direction, a seductive smile for Fintan, and a well-placed cuff to the ear for the nearest drunkard attempting to pinch her arse, Marta sailed off.

"I love her," Fi said as Noah hustled her out the door. "I want to be just like her when I grow up."

"It's a little late for that. You're almost twice her age, love."

"Shut your gob, Noah Riley!"

His lips twitched, but he did as she ordered.

FIONOLA'S WORRY for Patrick was like continuous nettle pricks under Noah's skin. Not because he was jealous—he absolutely was—but because her emotions were all over the place, and whatever she was feeling for the man was stronger than anything she'd believed she felt for him. That emotion was the main reason he'd given them his blessing and walked away yesterday after she kissed Patrick. Of course, she didn't need him to say anything or offer his approval, but he desired for her to move on without the guilt she was wont to wallow in.

As their trio walked up the hill toward Fi's home, he told them what he'd heard.

"Tadhg and Clara came for Jimmy earlier in the day." He gave her a sympathetic smile when she grimaced at the idea her father was too pissed to put one foot in front of the other to make his way home. "Your da's a good man, Fi. Just disillusioned by life."

"What did they say?" Fintan asked.

"Tadhg asked Clara if she'd heard back from the men she hired."

The air escaped Fi's lungs in a rush, and Noah reached for her when she swayed on her feet, cursing himself for his bluntness and assumption that she could handle whatever he happened to regurgitate regarding her family's conversation.

"Fi?"

"I'm grand," she croaked, drawing on whatever reserve she had to continue up the hill.

The look he shared with Fintan was half worried, half exasperated. Someone like Fionola Bohannon would never admit to what she perceived as weakness if she could help it.

"Yeah, and what did Clara have to say in response to her son?" Fintan asked.

"She informed him she hadn't yet, and appeared vexed by the situation."

"Oh, Mam," Fi whispered.

The distressed sound, along with her building angst, tugged at Noah's heartstrings. His empathic ability was working overtime on her behalf, and the Bohannons' betrayal of her trust felt personal. Fi was strong-willed, yes, but she was also intelligent and deliberate in her choices. Had Clara and Tadhg simply voiced their concerns instead of sending thugs to hurt O'Malley, they'd have gotten farther with their objective.

The cottage came into sight, and Noah felt a sense of impending doom so strong it stopped him in the middle of the road. Fintan and Fionola took another moment to realize he'd halted.

"Noah?" Fi's tone was concerned but distracted, and he recognized she was still obsessing over her family's part in all this.

"Something's off," Fintan said, cutting off Noah's reply. "The patriarch is here."

"Aye." Noah shot Fi a grim look. "I feel him, and he's not happy."

She took off at a run.

Swearing savagely, he followed. Luckily for him, his legs were longer than hers, and he caught Fi prior to her bursting through the door.

"Wait!" He kept his voice low despite his urgency. "Don't go in half cocked. You don't know what you're dealing with here."

Fintan held up a hand with a glare and snuck closer to an open window. Voices were audible, but only Tadhg's was raised in agitation.

"Kill him now, Mam, and be fuckin' done with it already. Fi doesn't know the bastard's here, and she'll not be missing him. With his scrambled brains, she'll think he deserted her, she will."

Noah clamped his hand over her mouth to prevent the anticipated explosion. An elbow to his ribs was her repayment. He grunted, but refused to let go.

"Stay calm and listen," he whispered into her ear. "Clara's not prone to swift reactions, and we've time to help."

After receiving her sharp nod, he released her. Of course, she followed up with a heel to his instep. No one manhandled Fionola Bohannon and got away with it. He'd have laughed if it wouldn't have given them away.

As they huddled on either side of the window, waiting for the scene to play out, Noah experienced the eerie sensation of being watched. Easing his head around, he scanned the area, seeing no one but feeling another life force in the general area. Closing his eyes, he drew on his limited magic and sent it through the Bohannon home.

Three. Where was the fourth? Shouldn't Jimmy be present, too, even if he was merely sleeping off his earlier imbibing?

Concentrating harder, Noah pulled his remaining power from his cells, picturing the invisible thread in his mind and sending it room by room. In the primary suite, he found Jimmy, slumbering. The knowledge almost caused him to recoil, but he pushed through and sent the thread into the room on the other side of the wall from where they crouched.

Tadhg's energy was like a live wire, as always, with Clara's more subtle in nature, but still containing irritation. For Tadhg or Patrick, Noah couldn't quite tell. When he reached for the third entity, he found none.

He did recoil that time and hissed out a breath. O'Malley wasn't soulless, so how was it he put off no energy signature? What the hell was happening?

Again, he sensed a watcher.

With one last try, he sent his feeler threads out toward the place where he suspected the person hid. They connected with a wall, similar to a magical force field, about twenty feet from their location.

"Sullivan?" he whispered with a hand signal toward the suspected watcher. "Anything, man?"

When Fintan sunk to the ground, eyes opaque and visage a blank mask, Noah gripped Fi's hand, prepared to drag her away.

"He does that when the Sullivan ancestors are imparting a message," she murmured. "He's all right."

"But I'm not. There's another here, and I'm not happy not knowing who it is."

"Where?"

"Twenty feet to your right." Although he looked that way, he didn't gesture, not wishing to give himself away if the cloaked person hadn't noticed them yet.

"It's Patrick O'Malley," Fintan said in a hushed voice, scaring the bejeezus out of Noah when his body convulsed and he rejoined the conversation.

Sharing a what-the-fuck look with Fi, Noah stared hard in the direction of the hidden figure. "How can ya tell?"

Fintan threw up his arms and waved a hand toward the window.

"The second sight, man. How the feck do you think?" he replied at a normal volume, but with his tone expressing annoyance.

"Show yourself, O'Malley," Fintan demanded.

Nothing happened. No shimmering light, no big reveal.

"Astral projection." Fi nodded as if it were an everyday occurrence, yet as far as Noah knew, it wasn't an easy thing to accomplish. "Patrick defaulted to it in the prison," she explained before turning to Fintan. "I'm assuming you muted our noise, yeah?" When he nodded, she said, "Can they see me if I stand up?"

"Sure, if they bother to glance out the window, but it will be a shadow only. Like a cloud passing overhead."

"Good." Climbing to her feet, she peered through the glass. "He's in there and speaking to them. Or part of him is." Her lips firmed and she came to a decision of sorts. One Noah would probably despise because he hated recklessness. "Can you guide me to him with your magic, Noah? Make sure I don't trip over or crash into anything?"

"What are you intending?" he demanded, not down for her putting herself in danger. "If Patrick has reverted back to a broken mind—"

"He hasn't," Fintan assured them.

Fi waved them off. "I'm going to break through his wall. If he's doing what I believe, he's likely in a trance and unaware we're here."

"Why wouldn't he just go inside?"

"He'd view it as too dangerous." Fi positioned herself at the corner of the house. "Astral projection is his fail-safe reaction to sticky situations, or so I'm learning. Ready?"

CHAPTER 28

After Patrick left Fionola with the Seer, he cut through the alley to the Black Cat Inn. Halfway to his destination, his grandson Aeden appeared with a message from Anu. He'd become a Receiver from a young age and had developed a special connection to the Goddess in recent years. If the boy was dodging his parents and lurking in alleyways, he had a damned fine reason.

"Anu said she blocked the Guardians, but you'll find the answer you seek at the Bohannon cottage," Aeden told him in his raspy voice. His grandson had been injured in a car accident, and although healed by the Aether, he'd never lost the strained quality whenever he spoke. It was endearing but strange, as if the boy was a two-pack-a-day smoker who drank whiskey in place of water.

Aeden's message indicated Patrick was the one meant to find the source and go it alone, though he couldn't begin to guess why. He needed to trust the Goddess had a plan for him.

Patrick ruffled Aeden's golden hair and conjured a slice of chocolate cake. "You'll be sure to hide evidence of this, yeah?

And brush your teeth when you're done eatin' it, or they'll rot out of your head, boyo."

"That doesn't happen to witches, *seanáthair*."

"You've proof of that?"

Aeden narrowed his eyes as if trying to decide if Patrick was pulling his leg. Finally, he shook his head. "No."

"Aye, better to be safe, then. Scurry along, now."

With deep affection, he watched Aeden duck into the back of the pub, cake in hand and a wide grin on his face. From the moment he'd met his grandson, Patrick felt abiding love for him, and it seemed Aeden experienced the same. Their bond had been swift and strong, and despite the fact Patrick tended to lose his patience with people, the child would never be one of them. Indeed, the boy had a calming influence on everyone around him.

He remembered when Carrick was the age of his son and how inquisitive he was, always asking, "Why, Da?"

Rose would become annoyed and seek to shoo him away, but Patrick had taken the time to sit him down and explain the answer in great detail, filling Carrick's curious mind to brimming and providing him with more things to consider. The pride he felt for his children was limitless. They'd all turned out to be a thousand times better than Rose and him combined.

"He idolizes you," Eoin said, stepping from the nearby shadows.

With a deep sigh of regret for all the years and opportunities missed, Patrick faced his youngest son. "He's a child and doesn't know any better."

"Aye." The hostility in Eoin's eyes was like the crossbow bolt to the chest all over again. "You shouldn't allow him to get attached. You'll be leaving again, I imagine."

"Aye. The Goddess has plans for me."

A cynical smile curled Eoin's lips, and his expression was dismissive as he pivoted to walk away.

"Eoin."

Shoulders stiff, his son stopped but didn't turn.

"I'd have been there for ya if I could've. I didn't leave of my own free will."

"Sure, and I know that," he said with a scornful glance over his shoulder. "I'm not a feckin' eejit, Da."

"Why do you hate me?"

With a hefty sigh, Eoin laced his hands behind his head. "I don't. Not really."

Patrick waited, hoping for clarification.

"I don't know ya, do I?" Eoin posed it more as a statement of fact than a question. "You breeze in and back out, causing the others nonstop worry. That's to say nothing of the people you abducted and kept against their will. But we're supposed to be okay with all of it while you collect more enemies?" Dropping his arms, he shook his head. "I've a wife, Da. I've no desire to see her hurt because some gobshite takes it into their head to get even with the O'Malleys. Moira's and Loman's evilness was enough to last a lifetime."

"And you prefer me to go, never to return?" Patrick wasn't certain how he'd managed to ask, considering the idea of it was torturous.

"No, Da. I expect you to be a better man and get your shite together so the innocents like Aeden and Brenna don't have to look over their shoulders all their lives."

"I'm after doing that today, son."

"See that ya do." Eoin didn't storm away as expected. Instead, he strode to Patrick and hugged him fiercely. "I don't hate ya, Da. And like I said, I don't know ya. But I want to."

Tears blurred Patrick's vision, but he'd already committed his son's handsome visage to memory. One day, he intended to be a father his sons could be proud of. Until then, he had business for the Goddess to perform.

"Your Brenna is a lucky woman," he said gruffly.

"Nah. I'm the lucky one." Eoin grinned. "She's shy most days, but when riled, she's fierce and the most beautiful thing I've ever seen."

"Happy looks good on you, boyo."

"It feels pretty feckin' grand, too."

After they parted, Patrick cast one last regretful glance toward the pub. He'd have liked to say goodbye to Fi, but he could feel the urgency building. Anu was getting impatient and tugging his cord.

He jogged upstairs and gathered his belongings, teleporting them to his flat in Galway. Once the task was completed, he stripped the bed and inspected the room for anything he might have left behind. Satisfied, he closed his eyes and visualized the place where he'd stopped with Fionola. His cells warmed to burning, and when he could take no more, he felt the cool, damp breeze from the countryside drift across his feverish skin. The view was technically as beautiful today as it was the first time he'd seen it, and yet not. Without Fi beside him, that charming sight was wasted on him.

Voices down the lane caught his attention.

Clara and Tadhg were positioned on either side of Jimmy, escorting him home.

"I'll not hear another word, Tadhg Bohannon, and you'll be mindin' your tongue, boy!"

"But Mam—"

Clara dropped her husband's arm to put her fists on her hips, and Tadhg staggered under Jimmy's full weight. "Sure, and what did I say that you didn't hear?"

Reacting quickly, Patrick voiced the first spell that came to mind.

"Goddess, hear my plea,
Assist me in this time of need,
Hide me from eyes who would do harm,

Allow me to view from a distance with calm."

A mist-like substance clouded his vision, swirling up and threatening to choke him. Practiced at not making a sound, he fought to endure. When next he could see and breathe without effort, he was standing in the Bohannons' garden by the back wall of the house.

Walking up the pathway was Clara and Tadhg, with the latter still whinging about all he'd suffered at Patrick's hands. Behind them, Patrick's body double approached, and the loud echo of sound he'd heard from across the yard disappeared. Everything spoken between the group became clear, as if he were there with them. A curious calmness settled over him as he watched his other self walk through the cottage door.

"Would you like help putting Jimmy to bed?" he asked.

Tadhg would've chewed nails, swallowed them, then shit them back out whole before accepting his assistance, and Patrick didn't expect him to, either. But his mother had raised him proper like, and the decent thing to do was ask.

After Clara and Tadhg returned to the kitchen, Patrick launched into his explanation of what happened, somewhat surprised the woman was willing to listen, considering what he now knew about her involvement with the men in the alley.

They were six minutes into a discussion when Patrick sensed the presence of others gathering outside, but he didn't dare release his spell to check who those people were. Certainly not when Tadhg was becoming more agitated by the second. It didn't help that Patrick had questioned why Clara hired hitmen to murder Fi and him in the alley by the pub.

"Kill him now, Mam, and be fuckin' done with it already. Fi doesn't know the bastard's here, and she'll not be missing him. With his scrambled brains, she'll think he deserted her, she will."

"Ach! That hurts, it does," Patrick replied dryly. "If I didn't know better, I'd think you hated me, Tadhg Bohannon."

"I feckin' do!" the man snarled, lips curled and blue eyes shooting fire.

With a shrug of indifference that wasn't feigned, Patrick looked at Clara. "Did you despise me so much upon meeting me, or has this fool talked ya into it?"

"Sure, and I can make up me own mind, Patrick O'Malley. I won't be needin' the likes of Tadhg or you to tell me how to feel, will I?"

In her fiery response, he saw the ghost of Fi, and the vision was so sweet that he smiled. "No," he agreed. "But I'd ask you to give your daughter the same respect."

With a nod, she acknowledged his successful parry, though her son was slow to pick up on the change in his mother's mood or the crafty gleam in her intelligent eyes. "Will ya leave her alone if I ask ya to?"

Patrick shook his head. "No. But I'll leave her alone if *she* asks me."

The truth was, he intended to leave her, regardless. He had restitution to make, according to Anu. Though he couldn't understand why he wasn't able to do it and still keep Fionola close. But he'd not tell the others that. They needed to understand Fi's choices were her own.

A shiver swept him, and he experienced her sweet touch, though she wasn't in the room. With a frown, he glanced toward the window, but only saw a rain cloud's shadow darken the grass as it drifted across the yard.

"That's not good enough! Tell him, Mam," Tadhg injected.

"It is for me," Clara said. Fatigue had crept into her voice, and she waved in dismissal. "Be done with it."

The disbelief on her son's face told anyone who witnessed it that he wouldn't be giving up anytime soon.

Patrick sighed, feeling tired and as old as dirt. Would the

conflict never end? When did he get peace? More importantly, did he actually deserve it after what he'd done when his mind was unable to determine imagination from reality?

"I'll say this and leave you to mull it over. My mind was damaged when I returned from the Otherworld, and no one—including me—figured it out until Fionola." Patrick stood and tucked in his chair, then rested his hands on the high back. "The Aether and two of his best healed me, and I aim to make it right. If you require my death, then, aye, I'll give it without protest." He studied Tadhg's belligerent face before meeting Clara's thoughtful gaze. "But don't put your daughter in harm's way again, yeah? That fecker almost slit her throat, and she's innocent in all of this."

"He didn't do what he was told," Clara replied grimly. "They were only to catch *you* unaware and alone."

"There is always collateral damage, Clara Bohannon. *Always*." He shook his head. "I should know, because I've turned your son evil."

"I'm not evil!"

"He was twisted by Loman," she said in agreement. "I've done nothing to help him, to be sure."

"I wasn't..." Tadhg trailed off with a frown. "He..."

Patrick infused understanding and compassion in his voice when he said, "I was there too, boyo. I heard what that gobshite said to all of you. How he blamed your incarceration on the O'Malleys." Hour after hour, Loman had played a recorded message throughout the cellblock. He'd droned on about how the O'Malleys were at fault because they'd stolen his magic and murdered him time and again. His claim was that he was only after syphoning their magic to defeat his greatest enemy. "After a while, it seeps into your subconscious, especially while you're sleeping. If you hear something often enough, whether it be true or false, you begin to believe that's the right of it."

"What *is* the truth?" Tadhg asked hoarsely. "Are you trying to say you didn't imprison us again?"

"No. I did it to all those on our original cellblock, and only because my bent mind needed to create a safe space to land. It sought the comfort of the familiar."

"You admitted it yourself, Tadhg. The lot of you ate like kings and had the finest bed," Clara pointed out, bless her. "Other than to keep you there, he did nothing to hurt ya."

"I wasn't after torturing anyone," Patrick added. "But the truth started two hundred and fifty plus years ago when the O'Connors stole the O'Malley magic. My children fulfilled a prophecy, and our power was returned to us as a reward. Loman O'Connor didn't like the drain of his, so he sought to replace it any way he could."

"We were all caught in your war," Tadhg concluded.

"His, but yeah." Straightening from where he leaned on the chair, he approached Tadhg. "I can heal ya if you've a mind to let me. Take away the hate and damage caused by both Loman and myself."

"This will heal me better," the man said, his visage screwing up and revealing his contempt.

Patrick caught the flash of light off the blade a second too late. When he glanced down in disbelief, it was to see a knife hilt protruding from his chest. Clara's gasp matched another, but he was damned if he knew where it had originated from.

She gasped again as his body dissolved into a burst of shimmering lights and the knife clanked when it hit the floor.

CHAPTER 29

Fionola's hand on Patrick's chest brought him back to his physical form. Shouts from the cottage sought his notice, but he only had eyes for her, as she did for him.

"How did you know I was here and cloaked? And how did you break through my ward?"

"Noah figured it out. He felt your energy." She smiled as she stroked his jaw. "As for the ward, you left it open for those who love ya, Paddy O."

"And you instinctively knew that, did ya?" he asked dryly, dipping his knees to accept her sweet, lingering kiss.

"Not if I'm being honest. Fintan told me just as I approached ya."

The door to the Bohannon home swung open, and Tadhg charged out.

"What happened in there?" she asked as she shifted to put herself in front of him, prepared to face off against her bull-headed brother.

"He stabbed me in the heart."

She gasped but didn't turn around, likely already guessing Patrick had astral projected into their kitchen.

"The bastard," she muttered under her breath, causing him to huff out a laugh.

"Don't be too hard on him, love. Remember, he went through hell."

"As did you," she reminded him over her shoulder. "But you're not stabbing people in the chest, are ya?"

He opened his mouth to say he wasn't above it, but Noah and Fintan joined them, creating a protective wall in front of him. The immediate realization that he'd acquired friends floored him. Patrick's entire life had been a one-man journey. Him against the world. Yet they were all willing to confront a self-righteous prick who was justified in his anger.

Gripping Fionola by the shoulders, he moved her behind him. "I'll not have you fight my battles, Fi." He held up a hand. "Before you think I'm being a chauvinist, it has nothing to do with you being a woman—you're fierce and capable—and everything to do with not putting someone I love in the middle of conflict."

Her eyes softened.

"Feckin' charmer." Noah shook his head. "If only I'd thought to say it that way earlier, I'd have saved an elbow to the solar plexus."

"You manhandled me, ya tool!" she retorted.

"*You did what?*" Patrick's temper exploded, and he raised his fists in preparation to pummel Noah.

Fi dove between them. "Not like that!"

"Far enough, boyo." Patrick threw up a hand and created an eight-foot wall of fire in front of the fast-approaching Tadhg, careful to only let the younger man feel the heat yet not get burned. It moved when he did, blocking his path. With his other hand, Patrick eased up Fionola's chin and focused all his attention on her wary eyes. "Explain it, please, love."

"The first time or the second?" Noah asked with a snort.

"Ya manhandled her *twice*?" His rage was at a fever pitch, almost blinding him to the concern on Fi's face.

"No!" She elbowed Noah.

"Make that three times." He rubbed his midsection. "You may want to rethink a relationship with her. She's bloodthirsty, to be sure."

"Noah, I swear to the Goddess, if you don't shut your gob—"

The two of them continued to bicker and fight like a couple of Tom cats with their tails tied together.

Patrick laughed. "Never mind. I've the feeling you got the worst of it, Noah Riley."

"You can believe it," his once-rival agreed. "And for the record, it was only a hand over her mouth to keep her from screeching when she heard Tadhg order Clara to kill ya. I feared she'd bring them running."

Fi's eye roll was adorable as feck, and Patrick lost the fight to hide his grin.

"Speaking of, the man's skin is scarlet. He's going to have a full-blown stroke if ya don't release him," Fintan said.

"Aye, it's time to cool him off," Fionola replied, opening her palms and pulling moisture from the gathering clouds to douse the fire and her thick brother with it.

As he gasped in outrage, dripping and looking like a drowned street rat, Tadhg's face grew redder still.

"He might suffer a stroke regardless," Noah muttered. "I'm amazed he hasn't, with Fi as his sister."

"Sure, and if you want another elbow to the ribs, craic on," she warned. Striding forward, she shoved her brother's chest. "What were you thinking by stabbing the man, ya feckin' eejit? On the day the Goddess was handing out brains, yours went missing!"

Crossing his arms, Patrick enjoyed the show.

"Jaysus, you're a lucky man, O'Malley," Noah said in a low voice. "She's likely to beat him bloody on your behalf."

"She'd do the same for you or anyone she cares about. That's our Fi."

"Ours? You sound like you're willing to be sharing, and I know bleedin' well you're not. And also, she has a say. Her choice is plain."

Patrick's desire to laugh died as he watched her. Anu hadn't said he could keep Fi and still make restitution. She'd said he'd become her consort, which meant he'd move on to a non-earthly plane, and he didn't know how to proceed without offending the Goddess.

"Your heart is heavy, and worry is eating at you," Noah said. "What am I missing?"

"I'll explain it in due time."

"You'll explain it now. Fi has five more minutes of her rant left."

With the understanding Noah knew her better, Patrick walked a short distance away from the siblings to avoid being overheard. When the other men joined him, he explained what Anu had decreed.

"Aye, and it's a shame another can't take your place, pretending to be you," Fintan said when he'd finished.

"Who would want to?" he asked, doubtful anyone would willingly accept his punishment for him.

"You've seen the Goddess, yeah?" Fintan shook his hand out like it was hot. "She could make a man forget his own name, willingly."

"Then *you* go."

"Ack, no! I've my own fate to avoid."

An unwitting laugh bubbled up, and Patrick stared at the Seer, waiting for an explanation.

None was provided.

"I'll do it."

They both looked at Noah in shock.

"I can take your place and pretend to be you for untold power."

"Why would ya want to?" Patrick eyed him with suspicion. "Especially for me? For the power?" He snorted. "Trust me, it's not all rainbows and kittens. And besides, your path to Fi will be clear when I'm gone."

"I've my reasons for wanting more power, but they're altruistic, to be sure." Noah cast a sorrowful glance Fionola's way. "I love her, aye, but Fi loves *you*. She deserves to be happy, and I'll do what I can to make it happen. So, if it means takin' your place, I'll do it."

"But I've got to be the one to make restitution. You've done nothing wrong, man."

Patrick's frustration was at an all-time high. He had less than twenty-four hours to tell Anu his intent.

"Talk to Fionola, O'Malley. Let her be part of your decision," Noah advised. "And if you believe I can help, call me, yeah?"

With that, he teleported away.

When Patrick looked toward the Bohannon siblings, it was in time to see Fi punch her brother square in the face. His brows shot up.

"Noah's going to be sad he missed it," he told Fintan.

"Aye, it was grand, it was."

<hr>

"Mam promised no more hitmen." Fi placed two cups of steaming tea in front of Patrick's whiskey bottle and settled onto his lap. "We'll need to keep an eye on Tadhg for a bit, but he'll cool down eventually," she added after pouring a shot into each of their mugs and handing him one. "He's always been high strung."

"How are your knuckles?" He hid a grin behind his first sip.

"Grand, after ya healed them." She examined her hand. "I knew Tadhg had a hard head, but I didn't realize the rest of his face was like granite."

Patrick laughed.

"I suppose now's the time for you to tell the truth of it, Paddy O." She turned somber eyes on him as she lifted her drink and sipped it. "Why did you pack and move your things here."

They'd relocated to Patrick's Galway flat to discuss their future, or lack thereof.

"Anu assured me the Witches' Council will look the other way, given the circumstances. She also gave me a choice, and I've got to do the right thing, Fi."

"What choice?"

"Become her consort to make restitution for what I've done. Or not."

Although she paled and her mouth tightened, Fi didn't react in any other way. "What punishment is attached to the 'or not' part of this?"

"I don't know, but I can't imagine it's good."

"Ya didn't ask?" She jumped up and slammed her mug on the counter, whirling to glare at him. "What kind of bleedin' eejit doesn't ask?"

"I was too torn up at the idea of losing you," he retorted hotly as he surged to his feet. "Was I supposed to be weighing all the options when my heart was being torn from my chest?"

"Yes!" Her expression softened, and she patted his chest. "Yes, love, you were. You can't make an informed decision without all the facts."

"It doesn't matter, Fi. I have to help those I've wronged."

"And how will you help them?"

"With the power she gifts to me. I'll be able to remove their pain."

Fionola shook her head and cupped his jaw. "We are the sum total of our experiences and the pain associated with it. You can't expect to take that away without removing their memories. Who will agree to having it done?"

"No, I'll give them a choice. I can ease their suffering like I was tasked to do."

A frown drew her brows together, and her troubled blue eyes turned thoughtful. "If you were given the assignment at the beginning, don't you possess the power to achieve it? Why do you need more?"

The remembered sensation of bashing his head against the wall struck him, and he stared at her in wonder. Why hadn't he come to the same conclusion?

He didn't realize he'd asked it aloud until she responded.

"You're too close to the problem. Sometimes it obscures the solution."

"Do you think it's as simple as me completing the first assignment?" he asked with a stunned shake of his head.

"Would it hurt to summon her and ask? Why does she want a man in love with another to become her consort? There's no offense intended here, Paddy O, but if she's not particular about the fact, why not choose the likes of Ronan O'Connor with his fine face and grand—"

Patrick pressed his palm over her mouth. "Don't finish that statement if you want to remain in a relationship with me. It's not that I can't agree. The man has a fine face and grand body, but I'll always be wondering if you prefer him."

Peeling his hand away and placing it on her shapely ass, Fi winked. "I'll state it plain, Patrick O'Malley, and you need to hear me. Commit it to memory, too." She cradled his face. "I love you. I want you. Only you. And I've not fantasized about another while in your bed, nor will I. You're the one for me if you'll have me."

His grin started and widened with every point she

hammered home. Gripping her ass cheek, he drew her against his full length, allowing her to feel the desire he felt for her that was never far from the surface. "Those words are the most welcome to reach my ears, Fionola Bohannon."

"And?"

He didn't pretend to misunderstand. "And I love you. I want you. Only you. I'm not fantasizing about another while you're in my bed, nor will I. You're the one for me if you always want me."

She grinned as she wrapped her arms around his neck. "That sounds like you've committed. What are you going to tell Anu now that she has to replace you as her companion?"

Sunlight flooded the room, bathing them in its warmth.

"I think she's fine with it," he said with sudden certainty.

The choice was simple. It always had been, and it appeared Anu merely wanted Patrick to recognize the gift she'd given him.

Hugging Fionola tightly to his chest, he raised his eyes skyward.

"Thank you, Exalted One," he said silently.

"You're welcome, Beloved."

The fragrant smell of clean ocean air drifted to him through the open window, and peace filled him, making him feel truly whole for the first time in forever.

Another realization hit him.

The Goddess had been watching over him all along.

CHAPTER 30

As Patrick approached Ronan, he noted the younger man's expression remained neutral, as if he were wary of what to expect from him. He couldn't say he blamed the man for his guarded behavior. Patrick had been a proper horse's arse to him in the past.

"I'd like to speak to you, if you've a mind, son. Will you walk with me?"

Ronan's silver gaze darted to where Dubheasa was laughing with Eoin and Brenna over something Fionola was saying.

"I'll not take offense if you tell me no. You owe me nothing."

"I'm not telling you no, but I am intent on signaling Dove should my body turn up in a ditch, the next village over."

His dry humor was something Patrick appreciated.

"Did you work out a code between you prior to arriving tonight?"

A quicksilver grin came and went, and Ronan's eyes showed barely suppressed laughter. "Sure, and if I tell you we didn't, you may get away with murder. If I tell you we did, I look weak, and that's no way for a Guardian such as myself to appear."

"I'm not one to tell another they're weak. If it weren't for you, I'd be lying bloody in that cell still."

A pained expression crossed Ronan's face. "I'm after apologiz—"

"No, son. You've no need." Expelling a breath, Patrick led the way outside the parlor doors to the edge of the terrace, with the assumption the other man would follow. His gaze landed on the spot where Fionola gave him a second chance after his mind was healed, and he took courage that if she could forgive him his sins against her, then maybe Ronan could, to a lesser degree. "I'm the one who owes you the apology, boyo."

He faced his daughter's mate and offered up a conciliatory smile. "You've been good to my family, saving them time and again, earning yourself the hatred of your family."

"Sure, but most of them hated me prior to my defection, so it wasn't so great a loss. The only one who never wavered was Ruairí."

"And Reggie."

Ronan's brows shot up. "You know Reg?"

"Aye. I know that day was a bad one for you, but you may recall, his was the cell diagonal from mine. There was many a time when we talked art, philosophy, and books. He was as good a companion as I could hope for, considering the situation."

"I'm surprised my father allowed conversation at all."

Patrick nodded. "He'd hoped to use Reggie as a weapon one day. He'd said as much to both of us, but your cousin refused to give him the satisfaction." He smiled in memory of Reggie's wit, and how, more often than not, he'd taunted Loman from behind the safety of his bars. "He knew your da couldn't retaliate without walking into the cell, and Loman feared going inside. Maybe he expected Reggie to trap him; your cousin is sure clever enough."

"He is." Ronan leaned back against the rail and crossed his long legs at the ankles. "Why didn't you capture him with the others?"

"He's a slippery one. And clever. The part of me in control at that time likely feared he'd see through the charade when I couldn't myself."

"Aye. There's a semblance of truth to that, I suppose." Ronan frowned. "But I've not heard from him in some time, and I'm worried for him."

"You shouldn't be. The man is smarter than all of us combined." Patrick smiled as he lifted his drink in a toast to the absent Reggie, but sobered as he recalled what happened the day Dubheasa confronted Loman. "If I know your cousin, he hasn't forgiven himself for his part in my daughter's death. How would he know she returned from the Otherworld?"

"Both Eoin and I sent him messages in the days following her return. He knows." Running a hand through his shaggy white-blond hair, Ronan grimaced. "He'll come around or he won't, but he's been informed none of us hold ill will for him."

"It's happy I am to hear it." Patrick settled back against the stone railing beside Ronan, and it allowed him to see his family as a whole as they milled about, laughing, eating, and making merry. 'Twas the one and only time Bridget agreed to shut down the pub for the night. "Will you forgive me for being an old fool?"

"There's nothing to forgive, Paddy. Your mind was not your own." Ronan straightened. "Why would I hold it against you? And to tell ya true, I wasn't a good man before Dove. Your family taught me what it was to be a decent human being. I owe them for their willingness to set aside their animosity, to forget that ridiculous feud, and for caring about me when I had no self love at all."

"Aye, but you've developed into a person anyone would be proud to call son, brother, cousin, husband... *friend*." Patrick held out a hand. "Can we be friends, Ronan O'Connor? Can you try to place your trust in me as I'm ready to do with you? Can we end this war for good this time?"

A smile curled Ronan's generous mouth, and the man was quick to accept the peace offering. "I don't make war on women, children, or incapacitated old men. You were lucky I knew about your injury, or this might've had a different outcome."

"You knew…What are ya sayin', boy?"

A twinkle sparked in the silvery depths of his eyes. "I'm sayin' a Guardian sees the truth if he looks hard enough *and* if he has the help of an Oracle and a Goddess to tell him what to expect."

"Ya fecker! You couldn't have told *me*?" Patrick demanded, aghast that others had seen the outcome long before it happened.

"You wouldn't have met Fi if I had." After sipping his scotch, Ronan sighed. "I've come to understand knowing and telling can have two vastly different outcomes. The Aether and the wee Beastie have taught me that. But Anu had her reasons for allowing you to do what you did, and she told me to let you have your head in this race."

"Her offer?"

"She'd no intention of punishing me in your place. She intended to see what type of man you were. If you'd defend or sacrifice me to her whims."

Patrick shook his head in wonder, thanking his lucky stars he'd said the right thing at the right time. "Why did she offer me the position of consort, knowing I love Fi?"

"Another test. And a bet, to boot."

"A feckin' bet? The hell you say! Who was she bettin' with?"

Ronan laughed. "Me. I said you wouldn't be swayed, and she said you'd feel the need to make things right."

"Ach! You lost to her, then."

"No. I won. You weren't swayed from Fi despite your sense of justice."

An emerald light flared in the shadowed corner of the terrace farthest away from the doors, capturing their attention.

The Goddess had joined the party.

Anu approached with a rolling walk meant to make a man's mouth water, but neither Patrick nor Ronan took note. They bowed their heads, prepared to take a knee when she stopped them.

"No need to be formal among friends," she said with an indulgent smile. "I've come to pay the wager." A sly expression curled her lips and caused the dimple on the left side of her face to flash. "Unless you'd like to double down, Ronan O'Connor?"

"Nah. The affection an O'Malley has for their mate is an unwavering thing, and a sure bet. I'll not be so fortunate against you a second time, my Queen," he replied, with all the charm of the Devil himself. The flirty smile he gave her caused pink to tint the Goddess's cheeks.

"Sure, and I feel the need to warn ya, if Dubheasa catches you smiling at another that way, she'd cut off your bollocks," Patrick said, shooting a glance at her and meeting her narrow-eyed gaze. "Ah, you're too late! And just when I was beginning to develop affection for you. It was nice knowing ya, boyo."

The others laughed, and a small smile, visible across the distance, curled his daughter's mouth.

"What did you win?" Patrick asked Ronan.

"Your undying happiness."

The Guardian's and the Goddess's matching expressions were a combination of indulgent and affectionate, with compassion thrown in for good measure.

"I don't understand. Why?" he asked Ronan.

"My *ween* loves ya, Paddy. So does Dove. My life is spent in service to them, with my ultimate goal to provide them everything their hearts desire." Ronan gripped his shoulder and gave him a little shake. "You're part of that. It'll make Dove content to know you're with someone who cares for ya."

"I misjudged you something fierce, didn't I?"

"You were worried for your family. That's understandable and forgivable."

Overwhelmed with the need to show him his gratitude but unable to voice it, Patrick embraced him. "Thank you, son."

"You're welcome, Da. I can call you that now, yeah?"

"Aye. I'd be proud to be your da, Ronan, me boy."

As Fi observed Patrick bond with Ronan, she smiled. Her understanding was the two of them had been at odds since the former discovered the latter was Dubheasa's chosen mate. And of course, with Patrick despising Loman as he had, it was natural the transference of that hatred would be visited upon the son.

"I owe you an apology, Fi."

She spun to find Bridget, remorseful and apologetic. "You don't."

"Aye, I do. I was cruel to you when you tried to care for Da."

Fi hugged her and was somewhat surprised when the other woman returned her embrace. Bridget was proud and exuded an air of aloofness despite her need to care for everyone. She didn't have the warm, welcoming vibe of Carrick's wife, Roisin.

"You were doing the best you could in a shite situation, Bridget. I'll not fault you for it." Fi smiled. "You're about taking care of everyone but yourself, and your protective nature isn't a bad thing, to be sure."

"I'm happy Da found you and that you're willing to forgive him for your island adventure."

Laughing, Fi glanced over her shoulder to find Patrick watching them. "That's a perfect way to put it. 'Island adventure.' And the truth is, spending time there with your Da wasn't a hardship. We had the best food, the softest mattress, and quiet time to learn about each other. I understand why his wounded self desired to return to the familiar."

"It wasn't a picnic for him in Loman's prison," Dubheasa said, joining their conversation. "Quite the opposite."

"Patrick lived in the shadows for his entire life. One way or the other." Fi shook her head, struggling to explain. "There is comfort in clinging to your old way of life, all the same. He told me it was why his mind revisited the past and sought to rebuild it. But I think his kind nature didn't want the others to suffer, despite putting them back in the cells, and he created a comfortable place for them to reside."

"It makes sense he'd do that. Da has always tried to make things better for others." Tears filled Bridget's eyes, and she sniffed, rapidly blinking them away. "He's a good man, Fi. I'm happy you saw that in him."

"Aye, me, too. He's protective while honoring my independence and acknowledging that I know my own mind. That's the best quality in a man, don't ya think?"

"I do." Bridget grinned as Ruairí wrapped his arms around her from behind. "I've got one of those grand fellas myself."

"I've been upgraded to grand from eejit. I'll take it and be happier for it," he quipped before burrowing his face against her neck and blowing raspberries against her throat.

With a palm shove to his head, Bridget laughed. "You play the *grand* fool, Ruairí O'Connor."

"Ouch, and didn't that pierce me heart?" He turned her to face him and dipped her low, staring down at her grinning visage. "Ah, *mo ghrá*. I'll play the grand fool for you for as long as you'll have me. This lifetime and beyond. You're my greatest love, you are."

And the woman Fi had believed to be standoffish melted into a puddle of mush right there, for all the world to see. Love was reflected back at her mate, and their twin looks of adoration could warm even the frostiest of hearts.

Eoin, bless him, whispered something to make Brenna giggle, which caused Fi to join in. Were they all a bunch of romantics? It was easy to be surrounded by so much love.

Cian draped an arm over Fi's shoulders and hugged her to him. "Welcome to the family, love. But please, don't let Da sing in me pub again, yeah?"

Piper's amber eyes were twinkling as she said, "Cian's ego can't take being upstaged."

"Sure, and you're right about that, Piper, me love. But only because it fires your passion for me when I sing to ya." He abandoned Fi to sweep Piper into his arms and waltz around the floor as he belted out a jaunty tune.

"I love this family," Fi said with a girly sigh she never believed was possible for her.

"Sure, and that's a grand thing, love," Patrick said from behind her. "We've all grown fond of you, as well." His arm encircled her waist, and he dipped his head, placing his mouth next to the shell of her ear. "But I can put these young 'uns to shame, if you've a mind to see."

"I would."

With a wave of his hand, the terrace transformed. Low-hung lights dangled from black wires, crisscrossed over the entire space and were dimmed to provide an intimate glow. The sound of a lively fiddle filled the night, lending energy to the air. Potted evergreen trees with beds of flowers dotted the tiles along the railing, and an eight-foot table strained under the weight of a banquet made for royalty. In the center was a chocolate fountain, and surrounding it were platters of fruit in every variety imaginable.

Patrick led Fi to the table and picked up a strawberry. After dipping it into the chocolate, he held it up to her smiling lips. Instead of feeding her when she opened for him, he coated her lower lip and leaned in to taste it, gently sucking the fleshy bit into his mouth. He drew back after a leisurely exploration, and his wicked grin told her he could indeed put the younger generation to shame.

"A dance or two before a ride?" he asked.

"You prefer to build my passion to a fever pitch?" she teased, allowing him to lead her to what served as a dance floor.

"Always."

EPILOGUE

SEVEN MONTHS LATER...

The majority of those abducted and imprisoned by Patrick were understanding of the situation after he explained it. Restitution came in the form of restoring their magic with that provided by Anu. Their original abilities were returned to them, along with a promise of protection in the future. If ever they found themselves in need, they were to reach out to Patrick or Ronan and, through them, to Anu. For the disbelieving, the Goddess herself had made a special appearance, ensuring Patrick spoke true.

A support group was formed and met monthly in Lucky's backroom to help alleviate the trauma Loman had heaped on them. Patrick took part in every discussion, taking care to allow every speaker to have their say, and encouraging anyone reticent to open up to healing. Before the meetings adjourned, they would all join hands and express their gratitude for surviving when others hadn't been so fortunate.

For the families of the deceased, each of them made a point to visit and to tell stories of their loved one's bravery in the face of Loman's sadism. With permission from Anu and Isis, Patrick erected a memorial on the island, creating a safe space for families to commune with those residing in the Other-world. Whenever it was safe for the veil to open and allow those on the other side to cross onto the Earthly plane, he was there, with Ronan at his side, and the two acted as gatekeepers, ensuring the well-being of all.

"Reggie's arrived. Just there," Patrick told Ronan.

His son-in-law's head whipped toward the area reserved for teleporting, and a wide grin nearly split his handsome visage. "I didn't think he would."

"Word's spreading about what you're doing here," Fi said from beside Patrick.

"Aye," Ronan replied with a nod before striding off to greet his cousin.

As they observed the two men hugging, Fi rested her head on Patrick's shoulder. "Tadhg's expressed interest in visiting."

"Sure, and I'll believe that when I see it," he muttered.

"Well, open your eyes, Paddy O. He's there, on the dock."

Tadhg's gaze scanned the surrounding area, and his grim expression revealed his acute discomfort. Returning to the island was difficult for all of them, but the more they did, the easier it became to see the prison was long since torn down and its horrific past buried. In its place, something beautiful was blooming. Bonds were forming and relationships were developing.

"You've paid your restitution, love," she assured Patrick, stretching to kiss him. "Keep believing in yourself and your mission."

"It's easier to do with you by my side, Fi."

Her self-satisfied smile filled his heart to full.

"Should we go greet Tadhg?" he asked. "The least we can do is meet him halfway, yeah?"

"No. He needs to seek you out this time. You've tried to make it right in the past, and he was a stubborn twat. Let him take the step."

As soon as the words left her mouth, Tadhg's attention locked on them and he headed in their direction. A wealth of emotion came and went across his face, with acceptance settling down for a spell.

"Have you heard from Noah," Patrick asked her as they waited for her brother to reach them.

"Just yesterday. He's spending his spare time with his brother and family."

"Good. No one should be alone in this world."

Fi grinned up at him. "As if you haven't been popping into his pub for a pint!"

Patrick laughed upon discovering she'd found him out. "He's an interesting man to talk to."

"You've a healthy attitude about life, all the same," she replied before turning to greet her brother.

After a breathy exhale, Tadhg held out his hand to Patrick. "I've come to apologize for encouraging Mam to hire those assassins. And to tell you, I bear ya no more ill will."

"That's mighty big of you," Patrick replied, tongue in cheek, but willing to accept the offer of a truce. "Come, I'll show you around."

"Will ya join us, Fi?" her brother asked.

From behind him, Patrick shook his head, hoping she realized he'd prefer alone time to patch the rift.

"I'll catch up with you before you go, Tadhg." She patted her brother's cheek. "I've duties to see to here."

With a hesitant nod, her brother fell into step beside Patrick. They walked for a bit without speaking until they came to a clearing.

"This is where our cellblock was located," Tadhg said.

His voice was deep from the emotion he struggled to suppress, but Patrick experienced them all the same. Anu had gifted him with an empath's ability to feel what others were so that he could better help them heal.

"We haven't decided on what to build here, yet." He met the man's cautious blue gaze, pleased to realize Tadhg's animosity was truly gone. "Fi and I were waiting to see if you had any ideas for it."

"Me?"

"Aye."

"Why would either of you care what I have to say?"

"Because you're her family, and she loves you, boyo. And also because your mam wishes you to find an outlet for your aggression."

Wry humor flared in Tadhg's eyes. "She told me to make nice with Fi or not come home again."

"Is that the only reason you're here, then?"

"No. Rumor has it you're doing good things. I'd a mind to see it for myself."

Patrick surveyed all he'd built, feeling a vague sense of satisfaction. "There's more to do, and I could use your help if you'd care to give it."

"I would."

"No more knives to the chest, though, yeah?"

The flush of embarrassment colored the younger man's skin. "It's sorry I am for me temper that day, and every day before it."

"You had the right, Tadhg. Loman put us all through hell, and those who survived have come out stronger. Or at least, are working on becoming stronger."

"If you'll have me, I'll be a member of your team and be glad for the work."

"We'll have ya. Have a look around the place and be thinking of what would fit best here." He noticed Tadhg's curious gaze stray to Reggie and Ronan, lingering longer on the former. "His cell was diagonal to mine."

"Aye. I know who he is."

"The O'Malley-O'Connor feud has ended, boyo. I'd not have it start up again if you're looking to settle a score."

Surprise caused Tadhg's jaw to sag as he shifted to meet Patrick's gaze. "No! It's not like that. I know Ronan and Reggie were innocent of Loman's wrongful acts. I've no need to seek revenge on them for something that gobshite did."

"Then what's your interest—Ah!" Patrick could be dull as a rock some days and had missed Tadhg's curiosity for what it was. "Would ya like an introduction to Reggie?"

"He's posh and too good for the likes of me."

"So you've no desire to know him better?"

A wave of longing swept over him, and he recognized it as not his own.

Tadhg was lonely.

"Tell me, boyo, do you like to read?"

"Aye. Every chance I get."

Patrick smiled. "Then I think you'll have a lot in common with our Reggie, to be sure."

AFTERWORD

Thanks for taking the time to read **_Highballs & Hexes_**! I hope you enjoyed Patrick and Fi's story.

As promised, I'm giving you the opportunity to vote _yay_ or _nay_ for more books in _The Unlucky Charms_ series. Of course, I'll only write more if the series meets the minimum threshold I've set for the YAY crowd. Why waste the time and resources if it's not what everyone wants? I'd rather spend it writing something else the majority of you will enjoy.

VOTE NOW
https://forms.gle/1c5jqZ4EhxonfvLb7

If you've no wish to weigh in on my ultimate decision, I understand. You can still stay current on information regarding this series along with my future book releases by subscribing to my newsletter.
https://www.tmcromer.com/newsletter/

Or if you prefer real-time text alerts to emails, we've got you covered! Simply send the word **JOIN** to **1-866-708-7124**.

Be sure to label us in your contacts as **T.M. CROMER BOOKS.**

Oh! I almost forgot!

I know most of you will be wondering about Noah's fate. I have plans for our beloved Aether's younger brother. Be sure to subscribe to my newsletter for future developments.

You can also find out more about Fintan Sullivan in his upcoming book ***THE SEER.*** Keep turning the page for a list of my stories.

BOOKS BY T.M. CROMER

Get your printable list here:

www.tmcromer.com/printable-booklist

PARANORMAL ROMANCE

The Unlucky Charms Series:
PINTS & POTIONS
WHISKEY & WITCHES
BEER & BROOMSTICKS
COCKTAILS & CAULDRONS
WINE & WARLOCKS
HIGHBALLS & HEXES

The Sentinels of Magic Series:
THE AETHER
THE DEATH DEALER
THE SEER

The Thorne Witches Series:
SUMMER MAGIC
AUTUMN MAGIC
WINTER MAGIC
SPRING MAGIC
REKINDLED MAGIC
LONG LOST MAGIC
FOREVER MAGIC
ESSENTIAL MAGIC

MOONLIT MAGIC

ENCHANTED MAGIC

CELESTIAL MAGIC

EVERLASTING MAGIC

CAPTIVATING MAGIC

The Thorne Witches: Happily Ever Afters Series:

ENDURING MAGIC

BOUNDLESS MAGIC

ABOUT THE AUTHOR

T.M. Cromer is a multi award-winning, best-selling author, who loves to craft wildly entertaining stories designed to keep you glued to your seat, turning the pages to find out what the hell happens next. She specializes in kickass heroines and the men who adore them.

Genres she writes include paranormal romance and romantic suspense.

Want to stay up to date on what's happening in the world of T.M. Cromer? Subscribe to her newsletter at https://www.tm-cromer.com/newsletter or text JOIN to 1-877-795-1526 to receive release news and promo alerts.

You can also join her VIP reader group on Facebook to chat with her, participate in polls, or just keep current on what's happening. Become a member today at http://www.facebook.-com/groups/cromerscarousers.

FOLLOW T.M. CROMER:

facebook.com/tmcromer

instagram.com/tmcromer

tiktok.com/@tmcromer

pinterest.com/tmcromer

amazon.com/stores/T.M.-Cromer/author/B011QK3WXY